Taming
my Prince Charming

J.S. COOPER

This book is a work of fiction. Names, characters, places, and incidents either are the product of the author's imagination or are used fictitiously. Any resemblance to actual persons, living or dead, events, or locales is entirely coincidental.

Taming
my Prince
Charming

Acknowledgments

Thanks goes out to all my readers for their support and love. I would also like to acknowledge several people who have really helped me with *Taming My Prince Charming*. Thanks to my editor Emma Mack for being so kind and patient, and thanks to Tanya Kay Skaggs, Katrina Jaekley, Stacy Hahn, Kelly Sloane, Cilicia White, Kathy Shreve, Lisa Miller, Chanteal Justice, Barbara Goodwin, Becky Warnick, Teri Salyer, Crissy Mackey, and Tianna Croy for all their help reading through the final document and providing me feedback. I love you ladies hard!!

As always, thanks be to God for blessing me and allowing me to write for a living.

I hope everyone enjoys the book!

Prologue

I always thought it would be romantic to be whisked away on a private jet by a handsome man. Only I never expected the man to be my professor. I never expected to be his fake fiancée. And I certainly never expected the games that he would play. Yes, being swept off of my feet is exciting and thrilling. However, it's not everything I imagined it to be. I've always dreamt about meeting my Prince Charming. I just never realized I'd have to tame him before the fairytale could begin.

Chapter One

"Welcome to Romeruis." Xavier's voice was light as we stepped out of the private plane. I didn't bother turning to look at him. His words on the plane had annoyed and thrilled me. I didn't know what was wrong with me. How had I, Lola Franklin, ended up in this position? "I want you to take this phone."

"What phone?" I spoke to the wind in front of me.

"The one I'm holding in my hand." He sounded short, and I ran down the steps a little faster. If he thought I was going to act like everything was fine, he had another thing coming.

"Lola," his voice rose, and I stopped. I didn't stop because of Xavier, though. No, I stopped because the tarmac was filled with about thirty different men dressed up in navy blue and red uniforms and they were all holding guns in the air. I'm pretty sure the guns were rifles with bayonets. There were about three different cars waiting for us as well, with three drivers standing next to each one. As soon as they saw Xavier, a young boy started blowing a trumpet and my mouth fell open. I'd never seen such fanfare at an airport before, but I guess I'm not used to being around royalty.

"Do not run ahead of me, Lola." Xavier growled into my ear and grabbed my arm. "Take this phone." His eyes bore into mine with an intense expression as he handed me the phone. I took it reluctantly and placed it into my handbag and watched a wide smile cross his face. "That wasn't so hard, was it?"

"What's going on here?" I nodded towards the crowds of people in front of us. "What's up with all the pomp?"

"My mother wanted to make sure that her firstborn and his fiancée were met with a royal welcome."

"I don't like the sound of that." I hissed at him. "This is making me very uncomfortable, Xavier."

"It shouldn't. You should be happy. Don't women like to be fawned over?"

"If it's real. This isn't real."

"I'll compensate you nicely."

"I don't want your money, asshole." I stopped and glared at him. "And if you mention money to me again or insinuate that I'm a prostitute, I will slap you so hard that you'll wonder if your face is still a part of your body."

"It was just a—"

"Do you understand me?" I cut him off and eyed him deliberately. "If I think for a second that you're associating me with being a whore at any moment, I will do something drastic."

"How drastic?" He smirked at me, his green eyes glowing with humor.

"I'll cut off your—"

"Xavier, there you are." Someone with a deep voice came running towards us and I looked down to see a handsome man grinning up at us. "We've been awaiting your arrival. Your mother is anxious to meet the woman who has stolen your heart."

My face burned a bright red as I stood there staring at the man. He reached out his hand to me and bowed his head, his blue eyes shining with excitement. "I'm Tarquin."

"Nice to meet you, Tarquin." I shook his hand and I could feel Xavier staring at us through the corners of my eyes. "I'm Lola."

"The pleasure is all mine." He grinned and then gave Xavier a look. "You nearly gave us a heart attack. Mama thinks that you've lost your head. They say that

Violeta has gone crazy. She can't believe it. She's going to flip a switch when she sees you. She thought that she—"

"Tarquin." Xavier frowned as he cut him off. "Enough."

"Oops, sorry." Tarquin gave me an awkward smile. "You must forgive me. I never expected to see the day when my cousin would get married."

"You two are cousins?" I was surprised. Tarquin, while cute, didn't look like Xavier at all with his white-blond hair and pale skin.

"Can't you tell?" Tarquin grinned again, looking carefree and happy, quite unlike Xavier.

"No, not really." I shook my head and smiled back at him.

"Go ahead, Tarq. I need to talk to Lola now." Xavier grabbed my arm and frowned. "Stop flirting with my cousin, it's so common."

"What?" I rolled my eyes. "What are you talking about?"

"I'm telling you to stop coming on to my cousin. You haven't cut off my balls yet. Tonight, I'll show you just how different Tarquin and I really are."

"What does that mean?" I could feel my heart pounding at his words. I tried not to stare at his handsome face and so instead looked at his muscular chest. That was a mistake. Staring at his physique only turned me on more.

"It means that when I fuck you tonight," he leaned forward and whispered in my ear, "there won't be any giggling going on." His tongue entered my ear and I froze. "It also means that when I'm done with you, you'll never joke about cutting any part of me off. Not when every part of me will be bringing you so much pleasure."

***

"So Lola, tell me what you do." Tarquin leaned forward with a curious expression on his face. "And how you met Xavier. The newspapers didn't really print much." He paused and looked at Xavier. "Aunt Henrietta is quite upset at you."

"She'll get over it." Xavier shrugged. "She has Sebastian to get it right for her."

"Sebastian isn't getting married as well, is he?" Tarquin's eyes widened with glee. "Oh, wait until I tell—"

"Tarquin." Xavier rolled his eyes. "Calm down. You're overwhelming Lola." He shook his head and turned to look at me. "How are you feeling, my dear?"

"Huh?" My jaw dropped. *My dear?* Really? He was really putting it on. I tried not to laugh in his face as I contemplated telling him just where I wanted him to jump from. I leaned back in the Rolls Royce that was escorting us to the royal palace. Everything felt so surreal. The chauffeur had bowed when he'd seen Xavier and me. He'd actually bowed. And then he'd held the door for me and everyone had waited for me to make my way into the back of the car first. It was so weird. I wasn't used to that. Guys back home didn't even hold the door open for me when we went on dates.

"Are you jetlagged?" His eyes danced as he mocked me and reached over and touched my forehead.

"Funny." I glared at him. "We were only flying for about two hours."

"I suppose you're still tired from Paris."

"Yeah, perhaps." I looked out of the window and stared at the city we were passing through quickly. "It's so quaint here."

"Don't let looks fool you. There's nothing quaint about Romerius." Xavier licked his lips slowly. "I'll be happy to—"

"Xavier, I hope you didn't tell her that Romerius is like London or even Berlin." Tarquin grinned. "She'll leave from boredom." He looked at me. "Not much goes on here. Everyone knows everyone, and let's just say everyone is excited to meet the famous Lola Franklin."

"Famous?" I grimaced.

"Oh, yes." He pulled out his phone. "I've had texts from all my friends asking about you. If you're as pretty as your photograph. If you're nice. If I think you're a gold-digger."

"It wasn't me who said it." Xavier interjected loudly and put his hands up. "Please say I'm safe."

"For now." I gave him a look and tried not to smile.

"What are you two talking about?" Tarquin looked confused and I shook my head.

"Don't worry about it." I laughed. "I can't believe people thought I was pretty." I smiled happily. "I've never thought I photographed particularly well. So that's nice to hear."

"Are you joking?" Tarquin looked shocked and then looked at Xavier with a curious expression. "Is she joking?"

"Joking about what?" I frowned and gasped as I saw a huge palace in the distance. "Oh my God, that's not where you live? That looks bigger than Buckingham Palace." I stared at the huge building as we passed through the ornate gold gates.

"Yes, that's my home." Xavier said dryly. "And Tarquin is shocked that you would inquire if you are pretty or not. We're not used to modesty in Romerius. Mostly every pretty girl knows she is pretty. So for him to meet a beautiful girl like you and for you to be shocked that others can see your beauty, well, it astounds him."

"I'm not beautiful, though." My face burned a deep red as I played with my hair and stared at them both. What was he talking about? As far as I was concerned, I was fairly average. There was nothing that screamed beautiful to me when I looked in the mirror. Granted there were days that I felt more pretty than others, but I'd never felt beautiful.

"Is she for real?" Tarquin spoke to Xavier but stared at me. "You're gorgeous, Lola."

"You think so?" I looked down, feeling embarrassed.

"Of course you are." Xavier frowned. "Your hair is silky and a deep, rich chestnut brown. Your eyes are warm and open. Your skin is smooth and your complexion resembles that of a juicy peach. Your body is curved like a sexy statue. You, my dear, are as close to a work of art as a woman can get."

"You're joking." I bit my lower lip and stared at him in confusion. "Right?"

"Why do you not believe?" Xavier's eyes narrowed.

"Most guys like girls with blonde hair, blue eyes, skinny waists..." My voice trailed off.

"That's a vision of beauty in America to some people." Xavier shrugged. "Yes, there are beautiful blondes and beautiful skinny women. However, no woman should think that they have to fit those three characteristics to be seen as beautiful. You, my dear, are a natural beauty." He picked up my hand and ran his fingers up my arm and then to my neck. "Here in Romerius, we value the beauty in every woman. And I'm a man who likes a bit of flesh on my woman's bones." His fingers went to my waist and then to my leg, where he rubbed my thigh. My body was on high alert as he touched me and I could feel a fire burning up in my legs.

"I'm not sure any woman likes to be told she has a bit of flesh on her bones as their stomach is being rubbed." I laughed. "But I'll let it slide."

"Xavier can be a bit of an ass, sometimes." Tarquin grinned at me again. "Don't mind him."

"Haha, I try not to anymore."

"Really?" Xavier moved closer to me. "Is that so, Lola?" His hand moved back up my thigh and slipped inside of my leg. The movement made me jump and he laughed. "Are you okay, my dear?"

"Stop calling me that." I hissed at him, and I saw Tarquin looking away with a smile.

"What else did my mother say, Tarq?" Xavier ignored me and put his arm around my shoulder. "And did Father say anything?"

"Uncle James just laughed." Tarquin grinned. "That didn't make Aunt Henrietta very happy."

"She's still in shock, I suppose."

"I thought you were never getting married."

"I'm not." Xavier snapped at his cousin and then realized his mistake. "I mean I never thought I was going to, until I met Lola. She took my breath away when I saw her. It was only when I saw her that I realized what I was missing out on."

I watched him talking and for a few seconds, I almost believed it was real. For a few seconds, I stared at his profile and thought all my dreams had really come true. Maybe he really did love me. Maybe I was the one he'd always wanted. *Yeah, Lola, and maybe pigs fly.* I chided myself silently.

"Once he saw me, he knew he had to have me." I spoke up and smiled sweetly at Xavier. "He knew that I was the one he wanted to marry." I reached over and grabbed his arm. "And we're going to go and get me a nice big ring tomorrow, aren't we?" I almost burst out laughing as his eyes narrowed at me. *Take that, Xavier. Two can play your game.*

"Sure, right after we get the toys."

"What toys?" Was he seriously going to talk about board games now?

"Oh, you know, the toys that will make your orgasms even more powerful." He grinned and grabbed my hand so that I couldn't remove it. "And maybe something that will make that other thing more attractive to you."

"What other thing?" I whispered, embarrassed that Tarquin was listening to us talk about sex. Had Xavier no shame?

"You know, the back—"

"Xavier!" I cried out loudly. "Enough." I looked at Tarquin surreptitiously to see if he had figured out what Xavier had been about to say. My face was burning a bright red. I was pretty sure that if cars could have seen me, they'd have thought I was a stop sign.

"Yes, my dear." Xavier leaned back and ran his hands through his hair. "Just wanted to make sure you were still excited."

"I'm not excited." I leaned over and whispered in his ear. "We need to talk when you're ready. And when I say, 'when you're ready,' I mean as soon as we're in private. I'm not about to just sit here and —"

"Oh, Lola." He turned his head, grabbed my face and kissed me hard. His lips pressed down onto mine, shutting me up as his tongue entered my mouth. I sucked on it eagerly as if I'd been in some sort of drought. His fingers made their way into my hair and he massaged my scalp as he sucked on my tongue. My body reacted swiftly and I felt myself relaxing as feelings of passion overwhelmed me.

"Get a room, you two." Tarquin's laugh brought me back to reality and I pulled back from Xavier, feeling slightly ashamed.

"I'm sorry." I turned to him with a red face. "I forgot you were there."

"It's fine." He shrugged, good-naturedly. "It happens to me all the time."

"Oh." I bit my lower lip, wanting him to clarify his response. Did it happen to him all the time generally? Or did it happen all the time when he was with Xavier? Did Xavier have a habit of making out with women when he was around? Not that I doubted that was true, but it made me feel incredibly sad and jealous. It was hard being the fake fiancée of a handsome bachelor.

"So what do you do, Lola? Are you excited to be in Romerius? Are you excited to meet Xavier's parents? What did your parents think of your engagement to Xavier? Did they think it was fast? Did they—"

"Enough, Tarquin." Xavier's voice was authoritative. "That's enough. You can ask Lola more questions tomorrow."

"Or in a week." I said sweetly, while wondering how in the hell we were going to extricate ourselves from this fake engagement in one week. I could already see the look of disappointment on Tarquin's face when we 'broke up.' I really wasn't sure why Xavier was having us go along with this plan. It made no sense. I know he'd said he was doing this to keep my reputation from being ruined by the tabloids, but I didn't really care what they had to say. It seemed like a huge over-exaggeration and I was slightly worried that a week with Xavier was going to be too much for me. Playing his fiancée would make everything seem real and I wasn't sure that was such a good idea. Anna would go crazy of course. She'd be excited for me and then she'd panic. Part of me wondered what Sebastian was thinking. He'd think it was weird, I'm sure. He didn't know that I knew his brother before the class, and he knew that I couldn't stand Xavier. We both joked about how pompous he was and what an arrogant jerk he could be. He'd think I'd gone crazy. I cringed as I realized that he might think I was some sort of gold digger. That made me feel sad. I really hoped he realized that there was more to the story than he knew.

"Very funny, Lola." Xavier stared at me for a few seconds and then he slowly brushed something off of my cheek. "Get ready, you're about to meet my parents. My mother is very astute and can be difficult. Don't let her overwhelm you."

"I won't, dear fiancé." I smiled at him sweetly.

"I do believe you're enjoying this." He shook his head and stared at me with surprised eyes. "I thought you'd feel out of your element."

"You don't know me very well then." I grinned at him and winked. "You don't know me at all."

"Why do I think that's the truth?" The car stopped then and he jumped out of the door and reached a hand in to guide me out. "Welcome to my home, Lola. Welcome to the Royal Palace of Romerius."

"Don't you mean our home, Xavier?" My eyes laughed at him as I made my way out of the car. "Isn't this to become my home as well?" I slid out of the back seat and gasped as I stared at the palace in front of me. It was even grander than I'd thought when I'd been looking at it through the window. There were trees and ponds framing the front of the building and every inch of grass was perfectly manicured. There were statues at the entrance to the palace and I wanted to run over and study them in more detail. Then I noticed two figures coming out of the tall black doors that made up the entrance to the palace. I knew right away that it was Xavier's parents, and it was in that moment that it suddenly hit me. I was going to be lying to a king and queen. The king and queen of an entire country. Oh my God, what had I got myself into this time?

"Ready, darling?" Xavier grabbed my hand and led me towards his parents. My throat dried up and I didn't respond. I had no smart response this time. Who could ever be ready for this?

***

His View

Lola's hands felt clammy as we walked towards my parents. I knew that it had finally hit her. There were no more jokes coming fast and furious from her mouth. She realized the enormity of the situation. I would have laughed if I hadn't been feeling so hot under the collar myself. I stared at my parents in front of me and I saw Tarquin running towards them excitedly. I'd underestimated how seriously the family would take the news of my engagement. I was angry at myself. I hadn't thought this through properly. There would have been better ways to whisk Lola off to have some alone time with her. This seemed like a very complicated way to get some hot sex out of her. I wasn't even sure why I cared so much. I'd already had her. And I was pretty sure I could have her again. There wasn't a woman alive who would turn me down.

"Xavier." My mother's face lit up as we came face-to-face.

"Mother." I let go of Lola's hand and stepped forward to kiss my mother. "You're looking well, as per usual."

"This is Lola?" She turned towards Lola and looked surprised. I knew that she hadn't expected to see a young girl, with unfashionable clothes and slightly frizzy hair. I'd thought about taking Lola shopping to get some new outfits before we came, but I wasn't sure how she would have taken it.

"Yes, Mama."

"Oh." She looked back at me with a disappointed expression. "Why did we have to learn about Lola from the newspapers?"

"Mama, I was going to tell you." I started and I could see Lola frowning at me. I knew that she wasn't happy with the lies. I was starting to feel uncomfortable with them as well. "Anyway, let us not argue. This is Lola Franklin."

"It's nice to meet you, Lola." My mother's voice was stiff as she shook Lola's hand.

"It's nice to meet you as well, Mrs— I mean Queen Romerius." Lola sounded awkward and I wanted to laugh.

"You may call me Henrietta." Mother's voice was monotone and I couldn't tell what she was thinking.

"Oh, thanks." Lola's voice drifted off and then my father stepped forward.

"I'm James." He grabbed Lola and pulled her into a bear hug. "I'm glad to finally have a daughter."

"Papa." I shook my head at my father's exuberant hug. "That's too much."

"Can I not say what I feel?" My father looked at me with a smile. "Does being a king mean nothing these days?"

"James," my mother scolded him. "Let go of the poor girl."

"I'm just welcoming her to the family." He shook his head. "I'm not doing—"

"Where's Grandma?" I cut him off. "I thought she'd want to come down and meet Lola."

"She's watching TV." My mother shook her head. "She's very disappointed in you, Xavier. She does not understand how you would not tell your family of this very important decision. We are all very disappointed, but I wanted to come down and meet Lola." She gave Lola a quick tight smile and then turned to me and spoke in our native tongue. "Who is this girl, Xavier? She doesn't even look like she is out of school. You expect her to become a princess and the queen of Romerius? Is this a joke?" she shot at me quickly, all the while keeping a smile on her face, so that Lola wouldn't understand what we were talking about.

"Mother, Lola is my choice for a wife and you'll just have to accept that." I retorted back at her, all the while smiling.

"I never expected to see the day you married and now, you say you're getting married to—to someone who looks like a poor orphan."

"I've never seen any rich-looking orphans, Mother."

"Don't talk back to me, Xavier." Her eyes flashed at me and I turned away from her annoyed.

"Is everything okay?" Lola looked at me with worried brown eyes and I nodded and reached for her hand. In that moment, I felt guilty. I felt guilty for subjecting her to what I knew was going to be a difficult situation, all because she was getting to my head.

"It's fine." I said finally, trying to ignore the way her lips teased me as she licked them quickly.

"Uh huh." She shook her head slightly and her eyes stared into mine with a question and taunt. She knew that it was not going smoothly.

"Let's go inside and show Lola her room." My father, ever the diplomat, spoke up.

"She's sleeping with me."

"No." My mother and Lola gasped out at the same time.

"Of course we are." I gave my mom a look and then Lola. "We're engaged."

"I don't care if you're engaged, it's not the proper thing." My mother shook her head. "I forbid it."

"Funny." I laughed. "You're forbidding it, Mother?"

"James, talk to your son." My mother gave me a look of disgust and then turned away from me. "I'm going inside. I've had a long day." She nodded her head at Lola and then walked inside.

"You shouldn't upset your mother, Xavier." My dad's eyes were laughing as he spoke to me. "It was a pleasure meeting you, dear Lola." He picked up Lola's hand and kissed it. "I better go inside and make sure your mother isn't too upset. I trust you can show Lola to her room, or whatever room she's sleeping in." He turned around and hurried back inside.

"You've gone and upset your mother." Lola's eyes flashed at me. "Now she's going to hate me."

"My mother is a drama queen, Lola." I shook my head and pulled her towards me. "Trust me, she'll be fine."

"I'm not sleeping in the same room as you, by the way. You've got to be joking."

"I never joke about such things."

"I'm not doing it." She looked at me obstinately. "I don't want your parents thinking I'm some sort of low-class tart."

"What do you care?" I leaned forward and ran my tongue across her trembling lips.

"It's not proper." She pulled back from me and I grabbed her around the waist.

"I don't care about what's proper."

"What do you care about, Xavier?" I could feel her breath on my tongue and lips and I froze at her words. Instinctively, I knew I cared about her. There was something about her that affected me more than I liked. She was getting to me. She was making me do stupid things. I didn't understand it. I didn't want her getting under my skin any more.

"I care about fucking you whenever I want, wherever I want." I pulled her body towards me and pressed my hardness into her. "That's what I care about."

Chapter Two

The gold trimming covering the bathtub shouldn't have surprised me, but of course it did. I'd never been around such opulence before. I took a deep breath and sat back on the toilet seat. I wasn't actually going to the bathroom, but I'd needed to escape from Xavier, and this was the only room I knew he wouldn't follow me into. Meeting his parents had overwhelmed me. Especially seeing the look in his mother's eyes. It had unnerved me. I felt really bad for deceiving them, especially as I didn't even know why

Xavier had set up this elaborate story. I didn't know why he hadn't just sued the tabloids for defamation or libel or whatever it was that celebrities sued tabloids for.

His mother had looked as I'd expected. Beautiful and cold. She looked aristocratic with her perfectly thin nose and high cheekbones. Her green eyes had pierced through to my soul, and she didn't have one hair out of place. I knew she hadn't been impressed when she'd surveyed my appearance. I reached up and touched the top of my head. My hair felt dry and I was sure it looked messy as well. I stood up and walked to the mirror. My face looked pale and washed out. I certainly didn't look like the sort of girl who had the ability to trap a prince. No matter what Tarquin and Xavier said, I was definitely not a Hollywood beauty, though I suppose there was a certain innocent, natural beauty to my looks.

"You alive?" Xavier knocked on the door and I froze.

"I'm fine." I called back, praying that Xavier wasn't going to overstep another boundary and walk into the room.

"Do you need anything?"

"I'm fine."

"No Pepto Bismol?"

"No." I shouted out embarrassed. "I'm fine."

"Well, you've been in there a while. I wanted to make sure you didn't have a scarred stomach."

"A scarred stomach?" I called out in surprise.

"Okay, maybe not scarred, scared."

"A scared stomach?" I started giggling.

"I mean an upset stomach."

"Don't worry, my stomach's not scarred, scared, or upset." I called out and walked to the toilet and flushed it, even though there was nothing in the bowl.

"I'm glad to hear that."

"I'm just going to wash my hands if that's okay with you." I called out and turned on the gold-plated faucets. Did they really need this much gold in a bathroom? It seemed ostentatious, but then what did I know? My family barely had enough money to pay the bills and get groceries every month.

"I'm waiting." His voice was soft through the door and I shivered. *Oh shit, here we go.*

"You didn't have to wait for me outside the door you know. It's unnerving." I snapped as I walked back into Xavier's bedroom. It looked like a display bedroom from a museum exhibit. "Your bedroom is crazy." I walked over to the four-poster bed and touched the thick wood.

"This bed belonged to my great-grandfather. It was hand carved in India. It was a gift to him from the English."

"The English?" I frowned. "I thought you said it was hand carved in India?"

"The English colonized India. Did you not know that?" He paused. "Oh yes, I forgot, you're an American."

"Excuse me?" I took a deep breath and was about to tell him where to get off.

"I'm not saying that to be rude." He shrugged. "I only said that to mean that English children would grow up with that knowledge because it was their country that tried to take over the world. The Americans haven't colonized anyone, have they?" He cocked his head and smiled. "Unless you want to talk about my heart. You've colonized my heart."

"Aren't you confusing your heart with your cock?" I said bluntly and he laughed loudly.

"Perhaps I am." He reached down and grabbed himself. "I'm still quite hard."

"That's nice." I walked to the window and pulled the curtain to the side. "That's some backyard." I stared out at the vast expanse of green lawns and flowerbeds. "It's beautiful."

"Thank you. We have ten gardeners. We have the Versailles Gardens of Romerius."

"I've never been to Versailles."

"I'll have to take you one day."

"That's okay. I don't need two fake engagements in my life."

"You can go as part of your first one."

"I think that's an awful lot to fit into one week."

"Well, it might be longer than one week." He shrugged.

"No." I bit my lower lip. "I have to get back to London. Xavier, why are you doing this?"

"I told you. I don't want you to be painted as a scarlet woman by the press."

"The press don't know or care about me." I rolled my eyes. "Date someone else and they'll focus on her."

"I don't want to date anyone." He walked towards me purposefully. "I'm not in this to date anyone. I'm in it to—"

"I know what you're going to say." I cut him off and gasped as he picked me up. "What are you doing?"

"Carrying you to my bed."

"Put me down." I struggled against him, my hands beating against his muscular chest.

"Will do." He dropped me on the bed and looked down at me for a second before lying down next to me. "Are you ready for me?" His fingers ran up to my heaving breasts and squeezed my nipple.

"Stop." I pushed his hand away from me. "This is so not appropriate."

"What's not appropriate?" He sat up and pulled his shirt off.

I stared at his naked chest and the sprinkles of hair covering his pecs. He reached over to me and I felt his fingers pulling up my shirt. I lay there without stopping him. I knew that I should say no, but I wanted him to touch me. My body craved his touch as my parched throat craved water.

"We should go shopping." He said as he stared down at me. "Sit up, so I can take your bra off," he commanded me and I frowned.

"What are you talking about?" I frowned at him. "Why should we go shopping?"

"It looks like you don't have many clothes? I think you've been wearing the same bra every time I've seen you. And frankly, it's not the sexiest bra I've ever seen."

"Excuse me?" My jaw dropped as his fingers slipped inside of my bra and played with my nipples. I squirmed on the bed as he teased my hardening nipples.

"I'm happy to buy you nice things. It will work out for both of us. I'd like to see you in a bra that —"

"I don't care what you want to see." I pushed his arm away from me and sat up and jumped off of the bed. "Every time, I say to myself, just give him a chance, he's not such a jerk, you say something that reminds me that you're a bigger jerk than I even gave you credit for."

"I'm a jerk because I want to buy you pretty things?"

"You're a jerk because that comment implies that my things aren't pretty."

"I'm not implying anything." He jumped up and ran his hands through his hair. "I'm telling you that your bra is ugly and your clothes aren't doing much to accentuate the beauty of your body. Your clothes should hug your body like a second skin, right now they cling onto you like a tick clings onto a dog whose blood it's sucking."

"What?" I shook my head and paused. "What are you talking about? You're calling my clothes a tick?"

"Whatever you took from that is your issue." He grabbed my waist and pulled me towards him. "Now, be quiet." His fingers deftly unclasped my bra and he yanked it off of my body. His lips fell to my breast and he took my nipple into his mouth and sucked on it gently before nipping at it with his teeth.

"Ow!" I cried out as his teeth bit down harder. "What are you doing?"

"I'm showing you that I can give you pleasure and pain." He looked up at me with teasing eyes. "Ultimately, I want to give you pleasure, but I will go through whatever modes of transport that I need to, to get you there."

"I think not— I don't want— Oh!" I cried out as his hand grabbed my other breast and his fingers squeezed my other nipple gently as he nibbled on the other one. It felt like the sweetest sort of pleasure and I could feel my panties growing wet.

"You don't want what?" He grinned as he pulled away from me and then looked at his watch. "We should shower now. Dinner will be served soon."

"Is that shower as in, we both shower or by ourselves?" I bent down and grabbed my bra as I spoke. I didn't know what to expect. I didn't know what to think either. I figured there was no point in lying to myself. I liked Xavier, I was attracted to him, and I did want to be with him. However, I didn't really know what that meant in the scheme of things. What did he really want from me? Who did he see me as? I wasn't stupid enough to believe that he liked me as a fiancée. I knew that he wasn't secretly pining over wanting to be with me. But what happened after a week? What happened when we had a week of fun and everyone realized that I wasn't really his fiancée? How would I feel if he discarded me like a piece of trash? I could lie to myself and tell myself I would be fine, but I wasn't so sure. I'd come into all of this with an idea and a plan, and now I wasn't so sure if I really knew what I'd gotten myself into.

"I'd love for us to shower together." He pulled his pants off. "And maybe a quickie in the shower before—"

"No." I shook my head. "You go ahead. I need to call Anna."

"Oh." He frowned. "I was very much looking forward to some sex."

"Yeah, I'm sure you were. That's not my problem."

"A lady doesn't talk back to a prince."

"It's a good thing I'm not a lady then, isn't it?"

"Why do you constantly challenge me, Lola? Isn't it tiring to always be so disagreeable?"

"Is that a joke?" I laughed at him. "There's no way you're calling me the disagreeable one."

"I think you'll find that I'm not disagreeable at all."

"You know what's funny?" I walked towards the bed and sat on the mattress and stared at him.

"What's *funny*?"

"Being here, in this palace with you is so much more different than I thought it was going to be. I thought that I'd be all overwhelmed by everything, but actually it's quite the opposite. Being here with you makes me see you differently. It makes me see you as an equal, okay, not an equal, but just like a regular guy."

"Regular guy?" He raised an eyebrow at me and I stared at his naked torso in front of me, trying not to run into his arms. Okay, maybe I had really worded that incorrectly. There was nothing regular about him. His body was toned and magnificent. My eyes followed down his chest to his abs and then to his hard cock that was standing to attention. I quickly looked down and stared at his muscular thighs and calves. How was it fair for him to have such a perfect body? He stood there looking so casual and cool, as if it were entirely natural for him to be standing there naked.

"You know what I mean." I swallowed hard. "I mean it's kinda hard to feel in over your head when the guy you're with is arguing with his mom, even if his mom is a queen."

"I'm glad you feel comfortable around me." He stepped towards me, his cock swinging, and I jumped up off of the bed.

"I need to make my call now. You better shower."

"Little Lola is scared of me." He laughed and stopped. "I guess you're not that comfortable," he murmured as he walked towards the bathroom.

"I guess you're not that big," I whispered under my breath as I pulled my shirt on. "What are you doing?" I squealed as I felt his arms around me picking me up and carrying me to the bed. He dropped me onto the mattress and then pinned my arms back next to my head as he climbed on top of me.

"Showing you just how big I am." His eyes glinted down into mine and I felt his cock rubbing against my body.

"Xavier," I gasped as he let go of my arms and pulled me up slowly. "What are you doing?"

"What do you think?" He winked at me and positioned his cock next to my mouth, rubbing the tip of it against my lips.

"I," I spoke and my eyes widened as I felt him push the tip into my mouth. I licked it, slowly delighting in the salty taste of his skin against my tongue. I wrapped my lips around him and he pushed himself slowly into my mouth, our eyes never leaving each other. I could feel myself starting to gag as he continued to push himself into my mouth. I opened up my mouth wider to see if I could take any more of him into my mouth when he pulled himself out swiftly and laughed and jumped off of the bed.

"I don't think you'll be making that comment again, will you, Lola?"

"You're a jerk." I sat up, my head spinning as I licked my lips.

"I guess you like jerks, then, don't you, Lola?"

"Whatever." I shook my head and he grinned at me.

"Go and make your call and I'm going to shower. Make sure to eat a hearty dinner, I have a long night prepared for us tonight."

"What do you mean a long night?" I frowned. "What do you have planned?"

"I mean a *long* night." He paused. "Or maybe you'd prefer me to say a *big* one."

"Oh." I flushed. "You're so crude. Did you just bring me here for sex?"

"I'd rather not answer that." He shrugged. "Or as you Americans say, I'll plead the Fifth."

"Uh huh." I walked over to my bag and opened it quickly and pulled my phone out as he walked into the bathroom.

"Lola!" Anna's voice was loud as she picked up the phone. "You're alive. What's going on?"

"You don't want to know," I groaned. "I'm in Romerius at the Royal Palace with Xavier."

"No flipping way."

"Yes, way. It's crazy. I even met his mom and dad, the queen and king."

"No flipping way!" Her voice grew even louder with excitement.

"And I met his cousin Tarquin. He came to meet us at the airport, but then disappeared when we made it back to the palace."

"Oh my God, Lola. You're in a palace."

"Can you believe it? It's so surreal."

"I cannot believe it." Anna's voice sounded a bit jealous. "You have all the luck."

"Anna, trust me. It's not luck. And it's not like he's fallen in love with me and wants to marry me. He just wants some hot sex."

"I want hot sex."

"Anna!"

"What? I'm just saying. Shit, I'd love some hot sex with a prince. Could you imagine what I'd tell everyone in Palm Bay, "hey, biatches, I fucked a prince? Who did you fuck, Johnny the head waiter at Applebees?"

"Anna." I giggled. "That's so bad."

"Okay, okay. Maybe they fucked Luke the shoe guy at Dillards."

"He was a sick fuck." I laughed, remembering the creepy middle-aged man who sold women's shoes in our closest mall in Melbourne.

"Do you remember that time I went to get heels for homecoming and we caught him sniffing my flip-flops?"

"Don't remind me." I shuddered.

"At least he gave me a discount."

"He should have given you more than 5%."

"I know." She sighed. "I miss you, Lola."

"I miss you too, Anna."

"I'm happy for you, though. I hope you know that I'm not being a sour bitch."

"You mean a hater?"

"I'm not being a hater." She giggled again. "Well, just a little bit. I want to meet a guy; he doesn't even have to be a prince. I want to be whisked somewhere. I want some hot sex."

"What about Sebastian?"

"Sebastian?" She laughed. "Yeah, right. He thinks I'm crazy after the first night we met."

"No, he doesn't." I lied. It was very possible that Sebastian thought she was a big creeper after her psycho behavior the night we'd all met.

"Lola, it's okay. You don't have to try and make me feel better. I'd think I was a psycho if I was him."

"I wish you could come out here."

"Why don't I?"

"I'll only be here for a week." I whispered into the phone. "Then Xavier will have no need for me."

"What?" Anna sounded pissed. "You are not going to really let this guy use you, are you?"

"I don't know what to do."

"Lola, remember this. You are beautiful. You are good. You are kind. You don't need no losers."

"Are you misquoting that movie?" I asked, laughing, but happy at her words.

"What movie?"

"*The Help*? You know that scene where she says 'you is this and you is that'?"

"'You is' isn't proper grammar."

"Anna, I swear. Sometimes you're so annoying."

"What? I'm an English major. It's something I pay attention to."

"Anyways, I just wanted to tell you I was okay and not to worry."

"I'm still going to worry."

"You shouldn't worry. I'll be fine."

"I can't help but worry. This isn't part of the plan. This isn't something you do."

"We all change and do crazy things."

"You're not the one who's supposed to do crazy things, though."

"I can't be boring Lola Franklin anymore."

"I think you lost that title the night you slept with Prince Xavier of Romerius for the first time."

"You're so bad."

"Actually, I think you're the bad one."

"No, I'm not." I giggled and then paused as I heard the shower in the bathroom stop. "Anyways, I really have to go. I think Xavier is about to get out of the shower."

"What? Are you sleeping in the same room? What?"

"It's a long story, Anna," I whispered.

"Don't tell me he's a prince, but lives in some sort of one-bedroom apartment or something? He's not a poor prince, is he?"

"No, Anna." I rolled my eyes. "His family is rich. Even the toilet is plated in gold. And I already told you I'm staying at the palace. You even exclaimed that you're so jealous I'm staying in a palace or something like that."

"So how is it that you two are sharing a room?" she demanded.

"He kinda told his parents we were engaged."

"WHAT?" Anna shouted into the phone.

"Anna, be quiet." I whispered. "It's a long story, but basically we were in—"

"You were where with who?" Xavier's dry voice interrupted me as he walked out of the bathroom, drops of water rolling down his body effortlessly. A towel was tied around his waist and he leaned against the door as he stared at me.

"Nothing. Look Anna, I have to go." I hung up the phone quickly and stared at Xavier. "I don't appreciate you eavesdropping on my conversations."

"You really didn't have a reasonable expectation of privacy talking to your friend in my bedroom, Lola." He shrugged and walked towards me. He shook his head back and forth and water drops went flying. He looked back up at me and I smiled at how crazy the top of his head looked.

"Reasonable expectation of privacy what?" I frowned and jumped up.

"Sorry, it's a term we use in the law."

"I thought you studied art."

"And law." He grinned.

"Well, bully for you." I rolled my eyes.

"A future king has to be knowledgeable in most things."

"What aren't you knowledgeable in?"

"Your mind." He said softly and his expression changed. "And the way I feel when..." His voice trailed and he shook his head. "What games are you playing with me, Lola? What magical powers do you have?"

"What games am I playing with you?" I gave him a look. "Is that a joke?"

"No joke."

"And I guess the only power I have over you is the power of the pussy." I said lightly and then slapped my hand to my mouth. I hadn't expected to say that out loud. "Oops, I didn't mean that."

"Sure you didn't." He stopped in front of me. "Maybe you're using your pussy to trap me."

"Xavier." My face reddened.

"What?"

"That word is so crude."

"You just used it." He rolled his eyes. "Did you not?"

"By mistake."

"Go and get in the shower, Lola. You're confusing me."

"I'm confusing you? I don't even really know why I'm here."

"What's there to know?" His voice was exasperated and he walked to the closet. "Do you have anything appropriate to wear to dinner tonight?"

"Appropriate?" I stopped at the bathroom door and looked back at him. "What does that mean?"

"Something a bit nicer than what you had on today? Something befitting the fiancée of a prince of Europe."

"Oh, because what I was wearing earlier wasn't nice enough?"

"You have to admit it was a bit scrubby." He shrugged. "I know you don't have money, but do you have to dress like you shop at, what's that store, Walmart?"

"Are you telling me you think my clothes come from Walmart?" My jaw dropped at his audacity. Was he really telling me that my clothes looked cheap? I knew I was being more indignant than I should be. To be honest, many of my clothes came from Target and Walmart, and I was proud of it. I was pretty sure I was smart, buying jeans for $15 as opposed to $1500.

"I'm just asking if you have anything nice to wear tonight."

"Sure." I nodded sweetly. *I'll show him.* "I have something really nice to wear tonight."

"Good." He nodded in satisfaction. "Now go and shower."

"Yes, boss." I mumbled under my breath as I walked into the bathroom, and I heard him laughing behind me.

***

His View

I tightened my bowtie and stared at my reflection in the mirror. I looked as I normally did on the outside. However, inside I felt a bundle of knots of confusion. Lola was confusing me. I'd expected her to be quiet and timid and impressed by my wealth. I'd expected her to walk through each room and mentally calculate how much I was worth. Well, that wasn't true. I didn't think she was after my money. She had so little care for money and status symbols. It was something I loved about her, yet I didn't know how she'd survive in my world. She'd be judged by her appearance and I'd be judged by her appearance. I sighed as I realized that I was thinking about her being with me in the long term. What did it matter to me if she looked like a model on the catwalk or a bag lady? It didn't.

I froze as I heard her coming out of the bathroom. I didn't want to look at her. I didn't want to feel that habitual need every time I looked into her eyes.

"Is this outfit good enough for tonight?" she said sweetly and I turned towards her. Her eyes were laughing at me as she stood there in a red dress with big ugly yellow polka dots. It was horrendous, and as I was about to ask her what she thought she was wearing, I realized that she was playing me. She wanted to get a rise out of me—and not one in my pants. I smiled to myself as I decided to keep my mouth shut. Lola would feel more uncomfortable than I would wearing that at the dinner table.

"It's beautiful." I smiled at her and watched as her face dropped at my words. Did she really think she was playing with an amateur? Her twenty-one years were nothing compared to my twenty-eight years. She was going down and I was going to enjoy watching it play out.

"You really think so?"

"Oh, yes." I grinned. "Are you ready to go down to dinner now?"

"Like this?" I watched as she swallowed hard and hid a smile. Yes, this was going to be very, very enjoyable.

Chapter Three

The room went silent as Xavier and I made our grand entrance. Unfortunately, I knew that the silence wasn't because everyone was in awe of what a great couple we made. I knew people were staring at me and my cheap dress. Why had I chosen to wear it? I knew I looked like an idiot. The dress was short and red with big yellow polka dots. It had been a present from my grandma one Christmas, and I'd packed it to remind myself of her. I'd never planned on wearing it. I would never willingly wear this dress, not even to my local grocery store back home, and Publix was certainly no gourmet market. I cringed as I realized that I was wearing the ugliest dress known to man in front of a bunch of royals.

"This is your seat, Lola." Xavier grinned at me as he pulled a chair out for me. "Next to me, of course."

"Of course." I wanted to roll my eyes and move away from him, but I already knew that I'd already made a spectacle of myself.

"Did you lose your keys?" Tarquin asked me curiously as I sat down. I could see everyone staring at me waiting for my response.

"My keys?" I looked at him curiously, and I could see a bright light in his eyes as he laughed at me.

"Your padlock keys?"

"The padlock keys that open your suitcase."

"My suitcase didn't have a padlock." I frowned and saw that Xavier's lips were trembling. "Why did you ask that?"

"Oh, I figure you didn't have access to most of your clothes." He looked down at my polka-dot dress and I blushed.

"Tarquin." Xavier's mother cut him off. "Don't be rude. I'm sure that must be the fashion in the United States, their styles are very different from ours."

"I thought the fashion there was short shorts and tight tops?" He grinned. "If it's not, then I don't want to go to the States next year after all. I'll just go to St. Tropez instead."

"It's not the fashion in the States to wear dresses like this," I mumbled, embarrassed.

"It's just Lola's style." Xavier grabbed my hand. "She's unique like that."

"I'm just trying to express myself." I smiled at everyone at the table, going around and making eye contact with each person. I realized that the only people at the table were Xavier's parents, Tarquin and us. The table was so large and there was so much food on it, that I'd thought there were more people.

"It's nice to express yourself." Xavier's father nodded. "Sebastian was like that when he was a teenager, always wearing those hippie clothes." He smiled at me indulgently. "Now can we eat, I'm starved."

"James." Xavier's mother pursed her lips. "You're not starved or starving, you must stop saying that phrase."

"No one cares, Henrietta."

"We care." She looked at him sternly. "And you never know when you might slip up and say it in public and then all the liberals will be on you and the family. The king says he's starving, what about the rest of us?"

"Mother," Xavier sighed, "let's leave politics for another day."

"You know it's true. Between you and your father, the press is all over us."

"Mother, you know that I'm sorry for what happened. I can't go back and change the fact that the paparazzi followed Lola and me. It's not like we planned this."

"But an engagement, Xavier, really?" She almost sobbed as she gazed at her son in disappointment. "You know that you were betrothed to—"

"Mother." Xavier's voice was sharp. "You're being rude. Lola is sitting right next to me."

"You're breaking my heart." She sighed melodramatically, and I looked down at the table. I'd thought that Xavier was rude, but his mother was even worse. Did they think that the fact they were royalty meant they could speak as rudely as they wanted to people?

"I'm sorry, Lola. Would you like for us to go out to dinner instead?" Xavier gazed at me and I could see a look of concern in his eyes. I wasn't sure if he felt bad for me or more annoyed at his mother. I was about to accept his offer when I realized just how bad that would look. Imagine going out to dinner on our first night. What would people think? What would his mother think? Yes, she'd been rude to me. But I knew I wasn't going to be helping matters if I left now. A part of me didn't care what she thought or what happened.

This wasn't real. We weren't really getting married, and I wasn't going to have to put up with her in a week.

"Come." Xavier grabbed my hand and attempted to pull me away from the table.

"No." I said loudly and firmly. "This is fine. I don't want to leave."

The room was silent for a few minutes as we stood there and I wasn't sure where to look. Tarquin's expression had changed to one of admiration and I knew that he had expected me to leave. It was then that I realized that the servants were standing by the door and by the wall, waiting for us to be finished.

"Mother, we're staying. You can let Edith know that the dinner service may begin."

"Always so bossy." She looked at Xavier indulgently. "Just like your father."

"I'm not bossy, Henrietta." James looked at her and he rolled his eyes.

"You used to be." She grinned at me, and I saw her hand going over to his knee. *What the—?* I was thinking to myself. Was she flirting with her husband at the table? No wonder Xavier was so straightforward with his want for sex. I knew that Europeans were meant to be a lot more open to the idea of talking about sex and even showing their interest, but I hadn't expected this. Especially not from the queen of ice.

***

Dinner was pretty quiet for the most part. I was glad that there weren't many people. I knew my dress would have been the talk of the town if there had been outsiders there.

"Would you have let me wear this dress to a larger dinner party?" I asked Xavier as we made our way to the bedroom.

"I don't know. It's not for me to let you do anything. Is it, Lola?"

"I don't mean 'let.'" I rolled my eyes. "Obviously it's not for you to *let* me do anything. I just meant, would you have attempted to persuade me to wear another outfit if you had known there were going to be more people there?"

"Why would I try and dissuade you from wearing your fashion? Clothing is also art, and I'm glad to see you expressing yourself."

"You're an asshole," I exclaimed. "Obviously a bright red dress with yellow polka dots is not how I'm expressing myself. What sort of expression do you think I'm making?"

"Well, red typically represents whores and yellow is used by advertisers to attract people to a product they are selling. So perhaps the outfit is expressing that..." He paused and looked at me and smiled. "Let's not talk about it. Tomorrow is another day and there will be a more formal dinner with a large group of people. I suggest you wear something you'll be more comfortable in."

"Why, I don't believe it. I do believe you just stopped yourself from calling me a whore." I laughed as we walked into the bedroom. "I never would have believed it."

"You can show me your thanks tonight if you want."

"How's that, then?"

"In bed?" He grinned and I groaned.

"You're really too much."

"It will be a way for us to christen our relationship."

"We've already had sex." I walked over to my bag and pulled out a pair of shorts and a t-shirt. "We don't need to christen anything."

"Well, this would be our first time as an engaged couple,"

"We're not even engaged." I walked to the bathroom and then closed the door. "In case you didn't get it, the answer's no." I shouted so that he could hear me as I changed my clothes.

"Sexy." Xavier was waiting for me outside the door as I vacated the bathroom. "I take it that those are the clothes you intend to wear to bed."

"You are smart."

"You've got a smart mouth."

"A smart mouth?"

"You're mouthy. Too mouthy for me. I've a mind to show you what I think should happen to women that mouth off at me."

"Oh, yeah? What's that? Do you want to wash my mouth out with soap?"

"No." He followed me over to the bed. "No soap. Though, I would like to put something in your mouth."

"You want to put something in my mouth?" I stared at him in confusion and then it hit me. "Oh." I blushed and then glared at him. "You wish."

"Don't tell me that you're going to be boring tonight?" He pouted as he walked to the door and locked it. He pulled out the key and put it on the nightstand next to the bed. "We can do anything we want tonight without fear of getting caught."

"All I want to do is sleep."

"That's a pity." He loosened his tie. "There are so many other things we could be doing."

"You could show me some of the paintings in the palace." I smiled at him sweetly. "That would be quite nice as well."

"You want to see the paintings?" He looked surprised.

"I was in your art class, remember. I like art." I yawned. "I wasn't in it for fun."

"I didn't think you were." He pulled off his shirt, and I gazed at his chest. I was finding it very hard to think as he took his clothes off.

"What are you doing?" My jaw dropped as his fingers went to the top of his boxers. "You can't take your boxers off."

"Why not? It's not like you haven't seen me naked before."

"Xavier. You cannot sleep in the nude."

"I think you'll find that I can." He grinned. "I can and I will."

"That's not fair." I stepped back.

"You can sleep in the nude as well. I'm not stopping you."

"That's not what I'm complaining about."

"Why are you being like this?" He frowned, looking annoyed. "Why are you playing these games?"

"I'm not playing games. What are you talking about? If anything, you're the one that is playing games."

"What do you want from me, Lola?"

"What do you want from me, Xavier?" I looked into his tense green eyes. "Honestly, I don't know what you want. I know you said you're trying to help me, but I don't know what this is all about. Why am I here?"

"Do you really want to know?" He stared into my eyes unblinking.

"Yes." I nodded.

"Sit down." He nodded towards the bed. "Sit down and I'll tell you everything."

***

His View

Lola looked up at me with wide brown eyes. I could see the curiosity in her gaze as she stared at me.

All I wanted to do was throw her back on the bed and rip her shorts and shirt off. She just didn't understand what she did to me. She didn't understand that the mere sight of her made me hard. She didn't realize that she had a spell over me. Of course, I wasn't going to tell her that. I didn't want her to know the power she had over me. I had to give her just enough information. I didn't want to scare her away. I didn't want her to know the real reason she was here. She was still too timid for that. I was taking a huge risk bringing her here. I wasn't sure how she was going to react once I introduced her to the circle. She might flee and ruin everything. I had to trust her. I needed to trust her. I needed her to be my next partner. I wanted to watch her face as I introduced her to a lifestyle she never dreamed existed.

"So?" She licked her lips nervously, and I tilted my head and just looked at her for a few seconds. I ran my hands through my hair and looked at her lips for a few seconds imagining it was my tongue tasting her and exploring the sweetness of her mouth.

"You're right, this wasn't just for me. It was for you as well."

"Okay? How was this for me?"

"I wanted you to experience the most pleasure you could."

"What pleasure am I experiencing when your cousin and mother are dissing me and my dress sense?"

"I'm talking about sexual pleasure."

"It's always about sex for you, isn't it?"

"Lola, I don't want to lie to you, and I don't want you to lie to me. This is all about sex for both of us, isn't it?"

"No." Her face reddened.

"Are you sexually attracted to me?"

"What does this have to do with anything?" She looked away from me and crossed her legs. I knew I was getting to her.

"We're here because we have an amazing sexual connection. We're here because I haven't had enough of you yet. I'm here because I want to take you on a journey—"

"Another journey?" She raised an eyebrow at me.

"Not a literal journey. I want to take you on a journey of the mind and soul. I want to take your body on a journey that you've never been on before."

"What are you saying?"

"Do you trust me?"

"No." She made a face and I laughed.

"I guess no one can say you're not honest."

"So what are you trying to tell me?" She leaned forward and frowned.

"Do you trust me?" I asked again softly and stared into her eyes, searching for an honest answer.

"I guess so," she said reluctantly, and I grinned and walked over and joined her on the bed.

"Lola," I sat next to her and grabbed her hands. They felt warm and soft next to my palms. "I'm part of a club."

"What club? The country club?"

"I guess you could say it's like a country club in that it's exclusive."

"Okay?" She looked at me curiously. "And?"

"And I want you to come with me to the club one day."

"I didn't bring a tennis racquet."

"That's not the working out we'll be doing."

"What?" Her eyes narrowed. "What do you mean?"

"You'll see." I studied her face and stopped talking. I knew she wasn't ready. I wasn't even sure I was ready. It would be crossing every ethical boundary I knew. I hadn't thought it out properly. It was risky involving her. I didn't know why I was so drawn to her or why I wanted her to be a part of this with me. I had to make sure that Sebastian didn't find out. Not that he really knew about the club. Only heirs to the thrones of different countries were allowed to take part. I didn't think he would approve if he knew about it.

I'd been a part of the club for a few years. I'd gone to see what it was about and then stayed for other reasons. I'd enjoyed going up until the last girl had blindsided me with her blackmail offer. I hadn't trusted anyone after that, but I felt Lola was different. I didn't think she would try and get one over on me. And frankly, I was willing to risk it. I wanted to experience the club with someone like Lola. I was excited just thinking about it.

Chapter Four

I was surprised that Xavier didn't try to sleep with me when we went to bed. He was every inch the gentleman, even though a part of me wished that he would have tried something. Not that I would have succumbed. I just wanted to feel like he couldn't keep his hands off of me. I was also more disappointed than I'd thought I was going to be at the fact that he had worn his boxers to bed. It was nice sleeping next to him and feeling him pressed up against me, though I knew it would have been nicer if he'd been naked. I woke up feeling tired and dissatisfied. I was sexually aroused and had been since we'd arrived, yet there was nothing I could do. Or there was nothing I could do and not feel easy. Even though we'd already slept together, I still felt like I had to keep my legs closed for a few days in Romerius. I didn't want him to think I was his plaything, to do with what he wanted. However, a part of me wondered why I cared. Wasn't I just playing games and wasting time? Would I regret never allowing myself to enjoy every hour of this week? I wanted Xavier. I craved him sexually. His body set mine on fire. He was the water to my ice, the heat to my flame, the secret to my pleasure. It hadn't helped that he'd told me he wanted me to join a club with him. I'd been so mad when he hadn't told me exactly what the club was. I wanted to know so badly. My mind was on all sorts of things. What sort of club was it? A part of me wondered if it had something to do with art. Was he going to fly me all over Europe so we could see different pieces of art? Maybe he really appreciated the fact that he'd met someone who loved art as much as he did. However, a part of me believed that it wasn't art that he was talking about. A part of me believed that the club was something darker and more nefarious. Some part of me was excited and scared by the possibilities.

"Good morning, Lola." Xavier's voice whispered in my ear as he distracted me from my thoughts. "Did you have a good night?"

"I did, thank you. You?" I opened my eyes and peered at him with a shy smile. I was immediately struck by how devastatingly handsome he looked in the morning. He had stubble all across his chin and his hair fell forward and covered his sparkling green eyes. It was so unfair, how could he look so handsome in the morning? I knew that there was no way that I looked like a tousled beauty. I was confident in the fact that my hair was a frizzy mess, my eyeliner was smudged, and I most probably had bags under my eyes from lack of good sleep.

"I didn't sleep well." He licked his lips slowly. "I had a most unfortunate problem most of the night."

"Oh?" I frowned. "What happened?"

"The problem lies in what didn't happen." He leaned forward and kissed me before grabbing my hand

and placing it on his hardness. "I've been hard since last night and I haven't been able to relieve myself of the problem. I kept waking up, wanting to pull your panties down and enter you slowly. I had daydreams of waking you up with my cock in your pussy and you crying out in ecstasy and pleasure as I took you in a state of almost sleep. You'd wonder if the bliss you were feeling was a dream or real life, and when you finally realized what we were doing was very much real life, I'd have you on the brink of the most intense orgasm of your life. I've been contemplating the look on your face as you cried out and gasped as you came. It hasn't helped relieve me of my hardness."

"Why didn't you?" I whispered, my body frozen and my panties feeling wet.

"I wouldn't do that unless I knew I had your approval and complete trust. I won't do that until your body belongs to me."

"Oh." I gasped as his fingers found my hardening nipples and pinched them. "What are you doing?"

"I'm touching you." He grinned. "Or did you not know what the act of one person caressing another was called?"

"Xavier," I groaned as his fingers made their way down my shirt and to my shorts. His fingers crept inside and slipped into my panties so that they were rubbing against my slit. "Xavier!" I gasped again and closed my legs, trying to stop him. He grinned at me, and the touch of him rubbing me only increased my pleasure. "Xavier," I groaned and opened my legs and grabbed his wrist.

"Yes," he grunted, his eyes filled with desire. He pushed a finger inside of me and I stilled. My eyes closed as I felt a wave of pleasure running through my body. "I said, yes, Lola." He groaned as he moved his finger in and out of me slowly. I was so overcome with pleasure that I couldn't speak. I didn't want him to stop. I just wanted to feel him inside of me. I didn't care if it was his fingers, his tongue or his cock. Every part of him felt fabulous.

Then he pulled his finger out of me and my panties and drew it up to his mouth. I watched as he sucked on it and licked it eagerly. "So wet and tasty, Lola. I guess you've been thinking of me as well."

"No." I blushed and shook my head.

"We could relieve each other of our misery." He smiled and winked as he continued to suck on my finger. "I could pull your panties down right now and enter you. I could fuck you hard for a few seconds and make you come. I could flip you onto your stomach and have you screaming out my name as you wondered where your body ended and mine began. I could give you pleasure in ways you never imagined receiving pleasure." His voice was deep and husky as he seduced me with his words. "But I won't. We will wait. We will wait for the perfect moment. And in that moment, neither one of us will be able to resist. Neither one of us will be able to stop. And it won't matter where we are. It won't matter who is around us. All that will matter is that we consummate our passion. All that will matter is that I will be inside of you and we will become one as our bodies fuse together in the magic of passion."

I stared at him with my heart beating fast. I was so horny I couldn't stand it. I just wanted to be with him. I needed to feel him inside of me. I needed to be possessed by him. My head felt light and I was slightly dazed. My whole body was impatiently awaiting his touch and takeover.

"Shall we get ready for breakfast?" He climbed out of the bed and I stared at him in disappointment.

"Will we be eating with your family?" I said after a few seconds.

"Just Tarquin." He grinned and walked to his closet. "My parents have gone to Parliament today. We'll have breakfast with Tarquin and then we will go shopping."

"Shopping?" I chewed on my lower lip.

"Tonight my parents are throwing a small dinner party for us. Let me buy you a dress to impress? Please." His eyes pleaded with me to just let it be. "You, of course, are welcome to buy it, though I daresay you'd rather keep your money for other things."

"I don't want you buying me things." I shook my head. "It makes me feel cheap."

"We both know you're not cheap, Lola."

"It's just icky. I don't want any of this to be about what you can buy me."

"What about I buy the dresses and you wear them, but I will still own them. That way I'm not buying the dresses for you as gifts. You can borrow them."

"If you're buying the dresses for you, does that mean that you'll also be wearing the dresses at some point?"

"No." He laughed. "Unless that is a fantasy of yours."

"Of course that's not a fantasy of mine."

"Well, feel free to tell me one of your fantasies and I will make it happen…as long as you make mine happen as well."

"I don't have any."

"I have one."

"Only one?" I laughed.

"Don't you want to know what it is?"

"I don't really care."

"Liar."

"Nope." I lied and rolled over. "I think I might try and sleep for another hour."

"My fantasy." He flopped back down on the bed and I felt his hands on my ass, squeezing firmly. "My fantasy." He whispered into my back as his fingers slipped between my legs and cupped me in my private spot before running back up my ass. "My fantasy is to take your virginity."

"I'm not a virgin," I whispered back at him and squirmed on the bed.

"Your anal virginity," he grunted, and I felt him pull my shorts down exposing my ass. I felt his teeth biting down on my butt cheek and then he licked down my crack. "I want to show you things you've never even dreamed of."

"Xavier." I jumped up off the bed and pulled my shorts up quickly. "What are you doing?"

"Don't worry, my sweet Lola. I wasn't going to take it right now. It's something you have to be willing and waiting for."

"Don't hold your breath." I stared at him in shock as my face grew warm. Did he really think that I was going to allow him to do me in the ass? I blushed just thinking about it. How could that give me any pleasure?

"You're over thinking it, sweetpea." He laughed as I looked up in shock. "I know you're thinking 'how did I know' what you're thinking, but it's written all over your face. I think you'll be surprised by just how much you enjoy it."

"I'm not talking about this now." I shook my head. "I'm not interested in you doing that to me."

"What are you interested in me doing to you?"

"I want you to tell me more about the club," I asked him and watched as his eyes glinted with excitement.

"I'm sure you do." He grinned at me. "But I'm not going to tell you anything else right now."

"When are you going to tell me?" I said, starting to feel frustrated. There was something about not knowing that made you want to know even more.

"Tonight. I'll tell you tonight."

"At the dinner party?"

"No." He grinned. "Afterwards."

"Oh."

"Don't be disappointed." He laughed. "Trust me, it will be worth the wait."

"We'll see." I rolled my eyes at him. "If it has anything to do with you trying to feel up or enter my ass, I won't be a happy woman."

Xavier's lips twitched as I finished talking, and I watched as he burst out laughing.

"What's so funny?" I mumbled as he pulled out a pair of jeans from his closet.

"Nothing, my dear Lola, nothing at all."

***

"Try this dress on." Xavier held up a deep red velvet dress with a plunging neckline. "I think you would look marvelous in it."

"Don't you mean you think you will look good in it?"

"Oh, of course." His eyes laughed at me. "I'll look just as sexy as you will."

"Uh huh." I grinned. "Though you'll have to get a smaller bra for your A cups."

"I have to admit that I'm glad we don't share the same bra size." His fingers crept to my right breast and he cupped it delicately. "I'm so glad that you're a D cup."

"I'm not a D cup." I brushed his hand away and blushed as I saw the saleswoman staring at us.

"Double D?"

"Whatever!"

"Triple D?" He grinned.

"I'm a C cup."

"A very generous C cup, at that." He winked at me and handed me the dress. "Now try this on and make sure you don't wear your bra."

"Excuse me?"

"The neckline is plunging." He shrugged. "A bra will not be appropriate."

"A dress that requires me to not wear a bra is not appropriate for me, period."

"Just try it on." His lips curled. "And try this one on as well." He handed me a slinky black dress with sheer lace at the bosoms.

"Are you joking?" I gave him a look. "Everyone would see my breasts."

"Just try it on."

"I'm not going to wear either of these dresses to your parents' dinner party tonight. No way, Jose."

"It's not for the dinner party, it's for afterwards."

"What's happening afterwards?"

"You'll see." He licked his lips slowly. "It's all part of the surprise."

"I don't know." I shook my head as my heart raced. "I'm not sure I'm down for any of this."

"Do you want to have the time of your life? Do you want to experience the rush of adrenaline that only extreme physical intimacy can provide?"

"Extreme physical intimacy?" I repeated. "What does that mean?"

"Wait and see."

"Fine." I grabbed the dresses and sighed, though inside I was feeling very, very excited. "But what about a dress for the dinner party? Or are you expecting me to wear the polka dot dress again?"

"You could wear anything you wanted to wear and I'd still want to fuck the living daylights out of you."

"Xavier!" My eyes widened at his vulgar talk. "That's not appropriate."

"When will you learn, Lola? I'm the least appropriate man you will ever meet."

"I think I've figured that out already," I retorted, and he laughed. I walked into the changing room, half suspecting that he was going to walk in behind me. I was pleased when he didn't, and I took my clothes off quickly before slipping on the red dress. I stared at my reflection in the mirror and gasped. The V-neckline was low. Really low. My breasts were practically popping out of the dress, though only the swell of them was exposed. I bit down on my lower lip as I realized how close to the nipple the material ended. A wrong turn or move and I'd be popping out. There was also a huge slit in the dress than ran all the way all to my thigh and exposed a lot of leg. The dress was sexy as hell and the red complimented my skin tone, but still, I was unsure.

"Are you ready yet, Lola? I want to see the dress."

"I guess, hold on." I sighed and opened the door slowly. I watched Xavier's eyes widen as I walked out. He stared at me like a wolf staring at a plump juicy pig he was seeing for the first time. I walked towards him and then back again. Xavier's eyes never left my body and when I stopped in front of him again, he nodded with a small smile on his face.

"This dress will be perfect for tonight." His voice was throaty and his eyes narrowed as he surveyed me again, with a pleased smile on his face. "In fact, it will be more than perfect." He nodded. "Now try on the other dress."

"Why?" I frowned. "If we both like this one."

"Do not argue with me." He turned away as the saleswoman approached us. I wondered what she was thinking. She'd been giving me jealous stares since Xavier and I had arrived at the store. I knew she was in disbelief that I was the fiancée. I was the one that had 'stolen' the playboy Prince's heart. I knew she didn't understand what he saw in me. I could see it in the narrowing of her eyes as I'd walked into the store. She was thinking to herself, *What does this girl have that I don't? How did she catch the heart of the Prince?* She didn't know that the engagement was a sham. Frankly, I wouldn't have put up with the sham if it wasn't for the very real chemistry that we had between the sheets. I wanted to experience the intensity of the highs he gave me some more. I wanted to ride the rollercoaster ride he wanted to take me on, only I was scared to admit it. How did you admit to yourself that you wanted a sexual relationship with a man you knew would never be able to commit to you? And how did you have a sexual relationship with a man that you knew in your heart and soul you wanted more from? I'd already made that mistake once. I'd given myself to my college boyfriend, fully thinking he was going to be the one. I'd only ever imagined myself with one man. I'd never been the sort of girl who needed to sow her wild oats. I'd never been the sort of girl who needed multiple men to tell me I was attractive. I'd never been the sort of girl who needed to see what it felt like being with other men. Part of me was glad that it hadn't worked out with any of my college boyfriends. If it had, I never would have gotten to experience the magnetic attraction and explosions that came with Xavier. Xavier was a man who knew what he was doing. He was a master of pleasure. He was my master of pleasure. I knew that I wanted to experience everything that he was willing to show me. I knew this was a once-in-a-lifetime opportunity. Only I didn't know how to admit it to him or myself out loud.

"Are you okay, Lola?" He touched my shoulder lightly. "You've been thinking about something for a long time."

"Oh, yeah." I turned around. "Let me try on the other dress." I hurried into the dressing room again and pulled off the velvet dress. I took the black dress off of the hanger and pulled it on. It fit perfectly and clung to my body. I patted down the skirt and then looked in the mirror. "Oh, hell no." I muttered as I stared at my clearly visible breasts. There was no way in hell that I was going to wear this dress anywhere.

"I'm waiting to see it." Xavier's voice boomed from outside the door.

"I'm not coming out." I muttered, picturing the sales girl's face if she saw me in the dress.

"Lola."

"I said no. There's no way I'm coming out of the changing room in this dress."

"Let me come in then."

"I don't know."

"Lola." He banged on the door. "Let me come in."

"Hold on." I sighed and opened the door slowly. Xavier walked in immediately and closed the door behind him.

"Look at me." He ordered me and I turned around to face him. His eyes fell to my breasts immediately and he grinned. "Sexy." He pushed me back up against the wall and pushed himself into me as his fingers ran to cup my breasts.

"What are you doing?" I groaned as he pinched my nipple.

"What do you think I'm doing?" He pulled me up against the wall and lifted the skirt of the dress up.

"Xavier!" I gasped as I wrapped my legs around his waist. "We can't do this."

"Why not?" He grinned and pulled my panties down. "We can do whatever we want."

"The sales girl is waiting on us."

"Who cares?"

"Xavier." I pushed him away. "No."

"You say that word entirely too much."

"I say it because you deserve to hear it."

"I'd rather hear yes."

"I'd rather say yes, but that doesn't mean anything. If you don't give me a reason to say yes, I won't."

"I give you a million reasons to say yes," he groaned and stepped back as my feet found the ground. "Get dressed. I'm going to take you to a museum."

"What about my dress for that party?"

"I'll have twenty dresses shipped over for you in your size. You can choose your favorite when we get in."

"That's too much money. You can't do that!"

"I'm a prince. I can do what I want."

"Whatever." I shook my head. "I'm going to change back into my own clothes now, if that's okay with you?"

"I'd rather you change back into nothing, but you're not really listening to what I say, are you?"

"Xavier, I don't know what power you have over other women, but you really don't have that power over me." I laughed at the annoyed look on his face. "I'm not just going to drop my panties when you say so."

"Pity."

"Yeah, it's a pity for you. I'm not impressed by your prince status. I know what an asshole you really are."

"You hurt my feelings, Lola." He clutched his heart. "How shall I ever survive?"

"Funny." I rolled my eyes at him.

"Was that not a joke?" He grinned and then winked at me. "You seem to be full of jokes."

"Get out, please." I pushed him towards the door. "I want to change now and no, I don't want you in the room."

"Fine. I shall go out and pout while I wait for you, like a temperamental little girl."

"Are you calling yourself a girl? Is there something you want to tell me?" I smiled widely at him. "First you were talking about wearing dresses and now you're using little girl expressions. Are you trying to tell me you're about to make a change?"

"A change?" He frowned at me and then I saw as his eyes changed and he got my joke. "I should take you over my knee and spank you."

"No, thanks. You'd like that too much." I laughed.

"I think it is you that will like it too much." He grinned. "And the day is young, there is still plenty of time tonight for you to find out how much you like being spanked."

"Yeah." I walked over to him and tilted my head up at him. "Let me tell you this. If you spank me, I will be spanking you, too."

"Oh?" Xavier licked his lips and he leaned in towards me and whispered in my ear. "I like it when you talk dirty to me, Lola. It turns me on."

"What doesn't turn you on?" I answered him lightly, and he laughed.

"Touché." He nodded. "When it comes to you, there isn't much that doesn't turn me on." He winked at me again and walked out of the room.

I leaned back against the door and sighed. I was in way over my head. I had no idea what I was going to do. If I was smart, I'd tell him that I wasn't going to be a part of this anymore. I'd tell him I needed to go back to London right now. This very instant. I didn't even care if I didn't get my bags. If I was smart, I wouldn't let another hour go by in his company. There was something so hypnotizing about him, and I was grappling internally over my lust for him and my worry for my own self-preservation. I just didn't see how this could work out for me. In any way. I didn't want to experience heartache, but a part of me wondered if it wasn't a small price to pay to have one of the most magical times of my life. I just didn't know if the pleasure was going to be worth the inevitable pain I knew was coming.

***

The chiffon dress fit me perfectly and I stared at my reflection in amazement. My hair was being obedient for once and looked silky and smooth. My makeup looked perfect, and I grinned as I spun around the room. I felt like a princess. Even if I was a fake one. My heart beat fast as I wondered what Xavier was going to say. He'd never seen me dressed up like this. I hoped he would be impressed, though I was sure he'd been with plenty of beautiful women in his life. I heard the door opening and I paused as he walked in. He stopped as he gazed at me. His eyes narrowed as he looked me over, and I couldn't tell what he was thinking from the expression on his face.

"Are you ready?" he said finally and turned away from me.

"Yes." I answered him, feeling disappointed. Did he think I looked bad?

"Okay, we need to go down in a few minutes." His voice sounded angry. "There are a lot of people you'll be meeting tonight. Do not worry if you don't remember their names, these are not people you'll be meeting many times."

"Okay, that's good to know," I mumbled and stared at him.

"Do you need anything before we go down?" He gave me another quick glance and I shook my head. Why was he acting like this? "Good, dinner won't be too long."

"And then we're going out afterwards?"

"I'm not sure." He looked at me again and pursed his lips as he studied my face. His green eyes looked annoyed and slightly dazed, and I wondered if he was okay.

"Are you okay?" I asked him softly.

"I'm fine," he snapped and turned away from me. "Are you ready?"

"Yes." I ran my hands down my thighs and took a deep breath. "Let's do this. Is there anything I should know?"

"Anything like what?" He turned back at me and frowned.

"I don't know. Things your fiancée should know that I don't."

"You know everything you need to know." He opened the door.

"We haven't even discussed the engagement or anything." I hurried out as we walked down the grand corridor. "How did you propose?"

"Figure something out." He shrugged and then laughed. "What a mess this is."

"We don't have to go through with it," I whispered, feeling extremely self-conscious.

"Go through with what?" He stopped at the top of the stairs. "We're not actually getting married, you do know that, right?" His eyes narrowed as he stared at me. "Or were you hoping for something else?"

"Excuse me? What's that supposed to mean? Am I hoping for something else?" My voice rose. "You're the one who made me come here to be a part of this farce."

"Fine, as long as you don't think this is going to end in a big wedding with you becoming a queen."

"I wouldn't want to marry a jerk like you," I hissed, annoyed. "In fact, I want to go home tomorrow. I'm done with this and with you. You can't just speak to me like I'm some sort of—"

"You look very beautiful tonight, Lola." His voice dropped as he interrupted me. "Very, very beautiful. I'm happy you're here with me. Fake engagement or not."

"I, uh..." I stared at him in shock. Had he really just said that? He thought I was beautiful? He was happy I was here? What?

"Let's go do this thing, yeah?" He grabbed my hand. "Let's go make our grand entrance. Everyone is waiting to meet you."

"That's what I'm afraid of," I mumbled under my breath as we made our way down the stairs. I could hear the sounds of violins and a piano playing. There were hundreds of people milling around the palace and I felt my stomach rumbling from nerves. We were so not prepared for this. Everyone was going to know the engagement was a sham.

"It'll be okay, Lola, breathe," Xavier whispered as we stepped into the hallway. He gave me his first real smile of the night. "Now, let's go and have some fun."

***

His View

I watched Tarquin's eyes widen as he stared at Lola in her dress. His expression held the admiration and appreciation I'd felt when I'd seen her. I hadn't been prepared for the gamut of emotions that had hit me when I'd seen her in her dress, and her small, hopeful smile had frightened me. I was not interested in falling for Lola. I was not interested in love. I didn't want my heart to tighten when I stared at her. Like now. She was smiling at Tarquin as if he were her fiancé. It irritated me. Didn't she realize that Tarquin might take her smile the wrong way? He might think she was interested in him. I grew angry just thinking about it.

"Lola, come." I grabbed her arm. "We need to talk."

"Hi, Xavier." Tarquin grinned at me and I ignored him.

"Where are you taking me?" Lola gasped as I pulled her out of the room with me.

"We need to talk." I hissed, annoyed at her. "You cannot keep flirting with every man you see."

"What are you talking about? I've not been flirting with anyone."

"You will receive a lot of attention tonight." I pulled her into a small bathroom and closed the door. "You cannot let it get to your head."

"Xavier, I was just talking to Tarquin. No one has been flirting with me. In fact, no one has even smiled at me aside from him."

"Trust me, the men are doing a lot more than flirting."

"What are you talking about?" She rolled her eyes.

"I'm talking about this." I grabbed the back of her neck and pulled her face towards me before I kissed her hard. She was hesitant at first, but then she kissed me back passionately. That was one of the things I loved about Lola, she was always so honest with her emotions and physical reactions. I knew her body craved mine just as much as I craved hers. Her lips sucked on my tongue and I pulled her dress up and squeezed her ass. I was pleased to feel that she was wearing a thong.

"Xavier," she muttered against my lips. "What are you doing?"

"Shh." I groaned and lifted her up against the wall. "Wrap your legs around my waist."

"What?"

"Just do it." I unzipped my pants.

"No, you've been hot and cold to me all day. You didn't even speak to me when you came into the room. I don't get you."

I groaned as I looked at the desire and uncertainty in her eyes. "I thought you looked beautiful. It took me back a bit. I'm sorry I didn't tell you right away."

"Everything—"

"Shh." I kissed her again and undid my zipper.

"Xavier, we can't—" she gasped as my fingers found her already wet.

"Bang against the wall." I grinned. "And argue with me."

"Argue about what?"

"Anything you want," I groaned as I pushed her back against the door and adjusted myself. "We want people to think we're arguing."

"Why?" she moaned as the tip of my cock pressed against her opening.

"Because we don't want them to know we're fucking." I bit down on her neck as I entered her and she screamed out in pleasure. "Hold onto me." I grunted as I entered her quickly. Her pussy trembled on my cock and I groaned as I slammed in and out of her. "Stop arguing with me." I grunted out and banged the wall and she looked at me in confusion. "Argue with me." I whispered as I slammed into her again.

"You're a jerk," she gasped and clung onto my back, her fingernails sharp through my thin suit.

"When will you listen to me?" I shouted and pulled her ass up to stop her from slipping down. "Fuck, I'm so hard for you." I groaned into her ear as I increased my pace.

"You need to listen to..." She broke off with a cry. "Oh my God." She moaned and banged the wall. "Xavier!" she screamed as I pounded into her. I grabbed her arms and pushed them up and held them back. Her legs tightened around me and she shifted and that allowed my cock to enter her even deeper.

"Do that again," I grunted as my hands squeezed her breasts.

"Do what?"

"Move your hips," I groaned and leaned forward to kiss her. She moved back and forth slightly and my body filled with heat and desire and the feel of her around my hardness. I increased my pace as I felt her pussy lips trembling. I knew she was about to come. I could tell it from the way her walls were clenching and holding onto my cock. I slammed into her a few more times and she bit down into my shoulder as she came hard and fast. Her juices poured over my cock as I kept up my pace, and within seconds I was coming inside of her, exploding like dynamite. I pressed myself against her as we both came down from our high, breathing heavily. I grinned at her and then banged the wall.

"Don't you talk to me like that!" I shouted.

"I'll talk to you how I like!" She grinned as she shouted back at me and slipped down to the floor.

"I don't care how you talk to me as long as long as you let me fuck you like that whenever I want to," I whispered into her ear.

"By day I'm acting as your fiancée and by night, you're treating me as your whore." She shook her head as she licked her lips and smoothed her dress back down.

"That's the best of both worlds, isn't it?"

"I don't know. It's not something I aspired to in life." She made a face at me and all I wanted to do was kiss her again.

"That's a pity then." I pursed my lips. "Everyone should aspire to have their world rocked at some point." I smiled at her small intake of breath and the red hue that rose on her face. "I mean, I didn't see you complaining just now."

"Ass," she hissed.

"An ass that wants your ass." I laughed and opened the door so we could leave the bathroom. There were people outside the door staring at us with curious expressions, but I ignored them and grabbed her hand and walked towards the ballroom. All of a sudden, I felt happier and higher than I had earlier in the day. Now that I'd finally been able to have her again, everything was right with the world. I grinned to myself at the thoughts of the new world I was going to introduce her to. I wasn't sure that tonight was the right night, but I was very excited to see how she would act once she realized just how deep and dark my kinky side could go.

Chapter Five

"We're going to have so much fun." Tarquin grabbed my hand as we walked to his car. "I can't wait for you to meet everyone."

"I don't know," I sighed and yawned. "I don't feel like anyone is going to like me."

"What are you talking about? Everyone is going to love you. Everyone wants to meet the girl who stole Xavier's heart."

"Uh huh." I smiled weakly. "I'm not sure I stole much of anything. And no one cared about me much last night."

"That's because they're older. They know how to hide it better." He laughed. "Trust me, they were interested on the inside."

"If you say so." I shrugged, thinking about the previous evening. After Xavier and I had made love in the bathroom, we'd gone to the ballroom and danced and then I'd been stuck with Tarquin for the rest of the night while he had mingled. I'd felt so self-conscious that I hadn't gone out of my way to look at or talk to anyone.

"So," Tarquin changed the subject and opened the door to a cute small red fiat. "I've got to know. What made you go for Xavier and not Sebastian?"

"What are you talking about?" I slid into the car and frowned. "I didn't go for anyone."

"Well, Xavier and Sebastian were both in the class, right? Just in different roles. And everyone knows Sebastian is much cooler and even more handsome than Xavier. And, well, he's closer to your age. Not that

I have a problem with your age, but I'm just so curious. How did you choose Xavier over Seb?"

"I met Xavier before class even started. I had—I mean, we had a connection before class even started. He didn't even know he was going to be my professor."

"Oh." Tarquin looked at me curiously. "I didn't know you both met before class started. Sebastian didn't tell me."

"You've spoken to Sebastian?"

"Of course, we're best friends." Tarquin grinned. "Did he not tell you? We grew up together. He wanted me to come to London as well, but I said no way. I felt bad when Aunt Henrietta made him go, but not bad enough to endure the pain and stress of more school."

"He seemed to be enjoying the class."

"I'm sure he was faking it for Xavier. He didn't want Xav reporting back to Aunt Henrietta and getting him into more trouble."

"More trouble?"

"Sebastian's not the best student. He's not dumb, but we like to have fun."

"What does that mean?"

"It means that last term, while we were meant to be studying for finals, we were in Monte Carlo instead." He laughed. "And let's just say that he lost about a hundred grand playing craps."

"Wow."

"Yeah." Tarquin laughed. "Aunt Henrietta flipped a switch, is that how you Americans say it?"

"I guess so." I laughed.

"I'm so glad Xavier let you come out with me today. After yesterday I thought he was going to be a punk."

"What do you mean?" I bit my lower lip, wondering exactly what Tarquin knew.

"Well, he was giving every guy that even looked at you death stares and then he said that no one should bother you and that you guys were going to go somewhere afterwards, but I guess you changed your mind. Why were you guys arguing, by the way?"

"You heard us arguing?" My face flushed as I thought about our 'argument.'

"We all heard you guys shouting at each other and banging the wall. I nearly came in to save you."

"Oh, you did?" My heart stopped as I thought about Tarquin coming in.

"Yeah, but I decided it was better for me to leave well enough alone. I was glad to hear you telling Xavier what you thought. Too many women just accept everything he has to say because he's Prince Xavier, heir to the throne."

"I think they accept it for other reasons." I smiled. "There is the fact that he's hot."

"Ugh, don't." Tarquin made a face as he pulled up to a park. "Sebastian and Xavier got all the looks in the family. I got nothing."

"You're handsome as well." I looked at Tarquin and searched his face to see if he was upset.

"Eh, no, I'm not, not compared to them. But it's fine. They got the dark devilish hair and the tall and buff physiques. I'm blonder than blond and skinny like a matchstick. If I wasn't a lord, I'd have no women."

"You're not skinny like a matchstick." I stared at his pale white limbs and paused. "I mean you're not Arnold Schwarzenegger by any means, but you're not a twig."

"Are you talking to me, baby?" His face deepened as he tried to imitate Arnold. "I'll be baacccck."

"Uh, okay." I laughed as we got out of the car. "My best friend Anna loves blond guys, she'd love you."

"Where is this best friend you speak of?" He grinned. "I need to meet this woman that loves blond guys."

"She's in London." I grinned. "Waiting on me to come back home."

"Tell her to come over to Romerius," he said eagerly. "She can come with Sebastian. That way she can fly on the private jet and won't have to spend money on a ticket."

"She has class." I laughed. "And neither one of us has a hundred grand to spend gambling anywhere. We both need to go to class."

"What are you going to do?" He frowned as he stared at me.

"What am I going to do where?"

"Now that you're marrying Xavier. Are you going to give up school?"

"Of course I'm not giving up school."

"How is that going to work then?"

"How is what going to work?" I scratched my head.

"When you're married, your place will be in Romerius, not in school."

"That's not something I'm worried about. We haven't set a date for the wedding."

"Oh, really?" He looked at me curiously. "Do you not know when you want to get married?"

"I haven't given it much thought."

"Maybe you should stick with someone your own age. Sebastian and I are just as eligible." He paused and I froze, wondering if he was coming on to me. "But I guess you have Xavier, so you don't need us." He laughed.

"So who are we meeting?" I asked him casually, hoping to change the subject as he was making me feel uncomfortable.

"Just some of my friends and some of Sebastian's friends as well."

"Why do you keep mentioning Sebastian?" I frowned as we walked into the gardens. "And do you guys normally hang out at the park?"

"No, we don't normally hang out at the park. Only when we want to enjoy the sunshine. And I didn't know that I was mentioning Sebastian a lot. Sorry."

"Nothing to apologize about." I followed him through the gate.

"Where did Xavier go today?" Tarquin asked me as he waved to a group of people about ten yards away.

"I don't know. He was gone when I woke up."

"Oh, okay." He nodded. "Let's go and have some fun."

He ran over to the group and gave a couple of girls a hug and then stepped back. "This is Lola, everyone. Xavier's fiancée."

"Hi." I smiled at the group in front of me. There were three boys and three girls, all looking at me with curious expressions.

"Hi." A tall blonde with beautiful big blue eyes stepped forward. "I'm Violeta. It's nice to meet you."

"Nice to meet you too." I froze as her eyes looked into mine with a stony expression that didn't match her tone.

"So you're the famous Lola." She looked me up and down and smiled sweetly. "Not what I expected. At all." She stepped back and then walked over to Tarquin and gave him a kiss on the cheek. "Where've you been, Tarq? I've missed you."

"My parents have me at the palace with Aunt Henrietta and Uncle James to help around the palace now that Sebastian's kicking back in London."

"He's so lucky. I can't believe they let him go." Another boy with dark brown hair spoke up. "I've been working at my father's law firm for the last six months. I told him that I needed time off to work on the band, but he just won't listen."

"Mother told me I need to go to Switzerland for finishing school." A girl with long red hair spoke up. "I told her there's nothing that needs finishing about me. She said that obviously there was because I didn't have a husband yet." She rolled her eyes. "As if I need a husband. At my age!" Everyone nodded their agreement and then looked at me for a quick second with an embarrassed smile.

"How old is everyone?" I asked politely, not wanting to be a bitch.

"We're all twenty and twenty-one, except for Violeta, she's twenty-three." Tarquin answered.

"I'm the odd one out." Her voice was sharp as she gazed at me. Her fingers played with her long blonde hair and she shook her head back and forth. "I'm not royalty, not related to royalty, and my parents don't have any money." She smiled at me. "You could say I'm the odd one out in the group."

"Don't be silly, Vi." Tarquin rubbed her shoulder. "You're the queen of the group."

"That's true." She grinned. I stared at her slender figure. She was wearing a pair of short white shorts and a flimsy black top that showed her flat stomach. She stretched and everyone watched as her top moved up her body, close to exposing her braless breasts.

"How did you guys meet?" I asked curiously. Violeta didn't seem to be the sort of girl who would normally hang out with someone like Tarquin.

"Well, I—" Violeta began with a huge smile.

"We met through Seb." Tarquin cut her off and grabbed my hand. "Come, let's go grab some food. Louisa's cooks make the best croque-monsieurs, and you just have to try one."

"Okay." I nodded and I could see that Violeta was displeased at being cut off. A part of me wondered what she was going to say. Maybe she had dated Sebastian and it had ended badly. Maybe that was the real reason why he'd gone to London.

"So how do you like everyone so far?" Tarquin asked me excitedly, his whole demeanor changed as we reached a wooden table filled with food.

"I haven't really met anyone. I don't know how I feel." I said as I reached for a glass. That wasn't technically true. I already knew that I didn't like Violeta, but I wasn't going to say anything as it would look more like petty jealousy.

"Oh." Tarquin looked disappointed. "Everyone's so excited you're here. We all want to get to know more about you."

"Get to know more about me or me and Xavier?" I said finally and paused for a second. "If it's the latter, I'm not sure they'll be getting the info that they need." I was starting to feel really annoyed. Was it really such a stretch that Xavier would be with someone like me? It was starting to feel quite offensive. Everyone was saying how lucky I was to get Xavier, but I hadn't really heard anyone saying how lucky Xavier was to have me. Granted, I wasn't a princess, but I thought I was a pretty good catch. I was pretty, I was fun, and I was smart. He was lucky that he had me as a fake fiancée. I'm not even sure that Xavier appreciated how lucky he was either, which made me feel even more used.

"I'm sure they want to know about you and also how you and Xavier met and all that good stuff."

"I'm not in the mood. I'm not going to be talking about Xavier and me." I shook my head and took the plate he offered me.

"Did anyone ask you to talk about Xavier?" A feminine voice said behind me, and I turned around. Violeta was standing there with a disgruntled look on her face. "You're not the only girl he's been with and I, for one, doubt you'll be the last." Violeta looked me up and down. "I'm sure that you're just a rebound for him as he's trying to get over his ex."

"What ex?" I said, and immediately regretted it when I saw Violeta grinning at me.

"He didn't tell you about his last girlfriend? The girl he wanted to marry?" She raised an eyebrow. "She's the reason why he went to London to teach." She smiled and ran her hands through her hair again before giving me an evil smile. "Oh well, least said, soonest mended. That's what you folks on the farm say, right?"

"The farm?" I frowned.

"Oh, you're not from a farm?" She looked at my clothes pointedly. "I thought that was why you had such poor fashion sense."

"You thought I was from a farm?"

"What other reason would you have for wearing those clothes?" She asked me softly and I froze. I realized she was trying to wind me up and insult me. A part of me didn't want to take it. A part of me wanted to slap her hard. That would take the satisfied look off of her face, but I knew that wasn't really something I could do. I knew that word would get back to the palace and everything would be twisted. It would become a story about me being violent and hitting some poor innocent girl. And that would be just another reason of why I wasn't good enough for Xavier.

"Violeta, leave Lola alone. She'll think you don't like her if you keep that up." Tarquin frowned at her and she shrugged.

"Oh, I guess we don't want her to think that now, do we?" She laughed lightly and leaned forward to give him a kiss on the cheek. "You know I'm just a little pussycat."

"Yes, I do." He grinned and I could tell from his indulgent look that he was enamored with her. He was definitely not someone I could bitch to about Violeta. I would have to call Anna when I got home. I knew she would understand.

"I'm ready to go whenever you are." I said pointedly to Tarquin. While, I didn't want to say anything about Violeta to him, I wasn't going to lie and pretend I felt comfortable being here.

"Oh," he looked disappointed, his blue eyes filled with concern. "You haven't met everyone yet."

"I want to go home. I can meet the others another day." I put my plate on the table. "In fact, I'm going to go and walk back to the car. Take your time eating, but I'd like to go home."

"We can go now," he sighed, and took a couple of quick bites of his sandwich. "I told Xavier that I'd take good care of you." He gave Violeta a look and she just stood there grinning. Bitch!

"Are you ready now?"

"Yes, let's go." He walked towards me. "Do you want to say goodbye to everyone first?"

"No, I have no interest in saying goodbye to anyone." I said and looked at Violeta. "Let's go."

***

I went straight to my room when we arrived back to the palace. I was glad that I didn't see Henrietta when we got back because I wasn't sure that I'd be able to deal with her particular brand of snarky right after meeting Violeta. I knew that I just needed some space. The car ride back had been completely silent and I was glad that Tarquin hadn't tried to talk to me about anything. It was obvious to me that he knew I was pissed. And frankly, he had to know why. Unless he was a dumbass, of course. Which wouldn't surprise me. I knew many men were dumbasses around beautiful women.

I was glad that Xavier was not in the room when I entered. I didn't want to deal with any of his sexual innuendos at that moment. I knew I was in the mood where I would go off on him at any moment. I didn't understand why he hadn't told me that he'd just come out of a relationship. Was that why he now didn't believe in love, then? Had his heart been broken? That would explain why he was such a jackass when I met him. If he was still reeling from a bad breakup, it would make complete sense. I just wished he'd told me. Another part of me now wondered if I'd been brought to Romerius to make his ex jealous. From what Violeta had said, it seemed like his ex had been the one to break his heart and not the other way around.

I curled up on the bed and closed my eyes. I didn't want to think about it too much. I was hurt and angry and upset. I could feel my eyes growing heavy with unshed tears. I felt my heart constrict as I thought about Xavier in love with someone else. I didn't want to think about Xavier as being a nicer, more loving guy to someone else. I felt green with envy, and jealousy consumed me. It was in that moment that I realized just how much I liked him. I wanted him to like me as well. I wanted him to fall in love with me. I wanted this to be real. In my heart I knew that was the real reason I'd come to Romerius with him. He'd grown in my heart without me being totally aware of it. He was the man who had captured my heart with his first kiss. Maybe even the first smile at the museum. Maybe that was why I'd put up with so much crap. I'd been fooling myself by telling myself I could have sex and no real relationship. I knew that now. Knowing that Xavier had been in a relationship and he'd loved her was breaking me inside.

"Are you sleeping?" Xavier's voice woke me up as I felt him shaking my shoulder. I yawned as I slowly opened my eyes and I realized that the room was now dark.

"I guess I fell asleep. Where have you been?" I sat up in the bed and frowned.

"I had some business, then I went to get you a present." He sat on the bed next to me.

"What present?" I stared at him eagerly and tried to ignore the pounding of my heart as he smiled at me. He was just so sexy. It wasn't fair.

"You'll see in a second." He grinned and stood up. He reached down and grabbed my hands. "It's time to wake up, sleepy head."

"I'm coming." I yawned and stood up.

"Go and shower. Tonight we're going to a ball, and you're going to wear your red velvet dress."

"Uhm, did someone make you the boss of me and not tell me?" I raised an eyebrow at him and he laughed

"Shower now. We have to leave soon."

"What about you? Don't you have to get ready as well?"

"I'm going to shower with you." He grinned.

"Uhm, no."

"Uhm, yes." He laughed and walked away from me and turned on a light. "It will save time."

"Fine." I relented quickly, actually quite excited to share a shower with him.

"Don't worry, there will be no hanky panky." He grinned. "Tonight we will have more than enough of that."

"You hope." I smiled at him. "Just because you got lucky last night doesn't mean you're going to get lucky tonight."

"We shall see." He laughed. "Let me show you your present." He pulled a box out of his hand and passed it to me. I opened it eagerly and pulled out a small plastic contraption.

"What's this?" I crinkled my nose.

"That's a vibrator." He grinned and stepped forward. "You'll wear it tonight under your dress and inside your panties. There are plastic straps that you'll slip up your legs to keep it in place. I have the controller." He showed me a small remote. "When I want to get your attention, I'll turn it on."

"What?" I frowned. "I don't think so."

"Why not?" He looked disappointed. "It'll be fun."

"I don't want you turning on a vibrator at your whim. I don't want to be having an orgasm while I'm talking to someone."

"I'll only turn it on when I want your attention." He smiled. "I promise."

"I don't know." I made a face as I looked at the small vibrator. "It just seems like it would be uncomfortable to wear under the dress."

"Please." He grinned, sensing that I was weakening. "It will make the evening more fun."

"I guess so." I sighed. "I don't really want to, but I guess it's fine. If you turn it on often, I will just take it off."

"And I don't want you to do that." His eyes sparkled with happiness. "That's settled, then. Shall we shower?"

Chapter Six

"We're flying in a plane to go to a ball?" I looked at Xavier, the shock in my voice obvious.

"It's easier We're going to a different country."

"We're traveling to a different country to go to a ball?" I shook my head as we walked up the stairs to the airplane. "This must be some ball." I said as I smoothed my dress down and took a seat. The vibrator between my legs felt odd and I shifted in the seat to see if I could position it in a way that wasn't so dead and center.

"It's not a ball like you're thinking of." He grinned as he stared at me. "It's something quite different."

"What do you mean?" I looked out the window as the plane started taxiing.

"Be patient." He grinned and then pulled the remote from his pocket. "Want to have some fun?"

"No." I glared at him. "You're not going to turn that on now. If you do, I will not get off of the plane when we land."

"Aww, you're no fun." He laughed and watched as I shifted in my seat. "Don't forget to put your seatbelt on." He leaned over and grabbed the end of the buckle and pulled it around my waist and locked it. He stared into my eyes for a few seconds before pulling back. "There we go."

"I could have done it."

"I know." He nodded. "But I wanted to do it."

"That's because you like to be in charge of everything." I rolled my eyes at him.

"Am I in charge of you?"

"You wish you were."

"Wrong." He grinned and pushed a button on the remote. I felt the vibrator moving slowly against me and I grabbed his arm and squeezed it tight.

"Xavier," I growled at him and closed my eyes. "Please turn it off."

"I will if you admit that I'm the boss of you tonight."

"You're not!" I called out and immediately regretted my comment as I felt the vibrator rubbing against me slightly faster. I opened my eyes and tried to grab the remote out of his hand. "Xavier."

"Pardon me?" He sat back smugly and held the vibrator up high. "What did you want to say?"

"Xavier."

"Yes, Lola." His fingers were about to push another switch.

"Okay, okay, you win. You're the boss of me tonight."

"Good." He grinned and turned it off. "Just remember that I will only turn on the vibrator tonight if I want to capture your attention."

"We'll be together, won't we?"

"Yes." He nodded. "But not all night. There are certain protocols at these events that we have to follow."

"What event is this?" I asked him again, feeling like I was being kept in the dark about something important.

"You'll see soon enough."

"I want to know now." I pouted, and he shook his head.

"Patience, my dear Lola. Patience."

"Whatever," I sighed, feeling petulant like a little kid. I watched as an air hostess brought us two glasses of wine.

"Would you like anything to eat, your Highness?"

"No, thank you, Ingrid." He took both glasses of wine and handed one to me. "Don't drink it too quickly Lola, I don't want you getting drunk."

"Then you shouldn't have given me a glass of wine." I took a large gulp. "You can't tell me how quickly I can or can't drink it."

"Lola." He frowned at me. "Don't be impertinent."

"Don't be impertinent," I muttered, feeling daring. I was annoyed that I had no idea where we were going. And I felt slightly intimidated to be going to a ball with a prince, when it seemed like no one was really fond of me. His parents' friends hadn't spoke to me, Tarquin and Sebastian's friends hadn't been super nice and I couldn't imagine that Xavier's friends were going to be much nicer or care anymore.

"Are you okay, Lola?" He turned towards me. "You look stressed."

"I just wish I knew exactly where I was going." I sighed. "I want to know what to expect."

"Lola, you need to relax. The not knowing is part of the fun."

"It's not fun for me. I want to know what's going on."

"We're going to a party. We're going to hang out. We're going to have some fun. You're going to meet some of my friends. It's just going to be a fun night."

"So we're flying on a private jet to another country just for a 'fun' night."

"It's going to be the most 'fun' night you've ever had." He grinned. "You'll see."

"I sure hope so." I took another sip of wine and sat back. "Fine, I'm going to try and relax and see what happens."

"Good." He sipped some of his wine and then he ran his fingers along the rim of the glass.

"So there is something we need to talk about."

"Oh?"

"We need to decide our names."

"Our names?" I cocked my head. "I'm Lola and you're Xavier, unless you've been lying to me."

"No, we need club names." His eyes bore into mine. "We don't go by our real names once we enter the party."

"Oh, fancy."

"We'll also have to wear masks."

"Masks?"

"Yes, I have one for you." He smiled and called Ingrid over with his fingers. She seemed to know exactly what he was calling her for because she brought a small black bag in her hands and handed it to him. He opened it and handed me a small gold mask to cover my eyes.

"This is like *Phantom of the Opera* or something?"

"Or something." He grinned. "More like *Eyes Wide Shut.*"

"*Eyes Wide Shut*? What's that?"

"It was a movie." He smiled. "But it's not important. Let's think of names."

"Uhm, you should call yourself Alpha because you think you're number one."

"I like that." He grinned. "I shall be Alpha and you shall be Omega."

"The end." I frowned. "Why are you the beginning and me the end?"

He grabbed my hand then and stared into my eyes. "I am the first and you are the last and we are together. You must remember that, Lola. No one else can come between us. At the club, you are mine."

"And you're mine?"

"I'm no one's." He shook his head, his eyes dark.

"How is that fair?"

"Life's not fair, but it is what it is."

"Whatever." I looked out of the window at the orange night sky and all I could think about was Anna and how I wished she was here with me. I needed someone to talk to who wasn't Xavier. Tarquin was someone who I liked, but I knew I couldn't tell him the things I wanted to talk about.

"You're upset again?" Xavier tapped me on the shoulder. "I don't mean to upset you, Lola. I'm a very honest guy. What you see is what you get with me."

"It's fine." I shrugged without looking at him. "I don't expect you to be any different."

"I'm not the sort of guy you take home. I don't want to be the guy you take home. You might not even realize it, but you don't want me to be the guy you take home. We have chemistry. I like you. You like me. We're having fun. Like I told you when I first met you, this isn't forever."

"I don't want you to be mine forever." I looked at him angrily. "And to be accurate, you said that 'this,' whatever 'this' is, was for one night. And it's become a lot more than one night."

"This isn't love, you know that, right?"

"What are you talking about?" I laughed, though inside I could feel the beginning of my heart breaking.

"I don't know," he sighed, and his expression changed. "I'll be honest with you, Lola. I don't know what I'm feeling. And that upsets me sometimes. I don't want you to think that I'm leading you astray. I want you to be here. I want us to experience this passion together, but I don't want you to get the wrong impression. I'm not a guy who commits."

"Why create a fake engagement, then?"

"I don't know." He sighed. "It was a rash decision, one I don't fully understand."

"I guess we both don't understand together." I offered him a weak smile. I felt my heart softening at the expression on his face. This was vulnerable Xavier, a Xavier I hadn't seen before.

"It should be easy for me," he sighed. "Everyone sees me as this man who has it all figured out."

"Maybe that's because that's what you portray."

"Perhaps." He nodded. "I'm human like everyone else. My feelings get hurt. My heart breaks. My ego becomes bruised. I feel pain. I feel happiness. I feel sadness. I'm confused, and I'm also one hundred percent in control of my emotions at any given time."

"So you're human, then?" I bit my lower lip and sighed. "Why'd you have to go and act all human when

I was ready to call you some sort of emotionless robot?"

"You're unlike every girl I've known and met, Lola. We shouldn't be compatible. We're from two different worlds, yet somehow this works. Somehow you know just what to say to put me in my place and remind me that I'm not a god."

"Or a demi-god either," I added.

"Yes, I'm just a human being."

"Quite a rude human being as well. You've been really quite rude to me."

"You think so?" He raised an eyebrow at me and smiled.

"I more than think so. You basically insinuated I was a whore."

"But still I found you in my bed."

"Only because..." I glared at him and stopped talking.

"Only because you found my body totally irresistible." He laughed. "You couldn't keep your hands off me."

"Yes, I could and can."

"Fine." He reached over and ran his hands down the V-neck of my dress. "I can't keep my hands off your porcelain skin. I can feel your heart beating through my fingertips. I want to be inside of you right now." He leaned towards me. "I want my tongue to be nestled up under your dress where your vibrator sits patiently, ready and waiting to bring you to orgasm whenever I please."

"You're obsessed with sex," I breathed out, feeling horny as I imagined him licking up my juices.

"No, my dear Lola. I'm obsessed with you."

***

The plane landed about an hour later, and a limousine was waiting for us at the private airport.

"Where are we?" I asked curiously as I looked out of the window at the tall dark trees.

"We are in Delmar."

"Where?"

"It's a small country that was founded a thousand years ago."

"It's not very famous."

"That's how Casper and his family like it."

"Who is Casper?"

"You don't know Casper?"

"Not unless he's Casper the Friendly Ghost."

"Casper is the crown prince of Delmar," he said softly, and my body began to tremble with nerves. How was I going to act around another prince?

"In fact, all the men at the party are princes. I think I told you that before, did I not?" he continued.

"I'm not sure." My jaw dropped as we pulled up to a castle on a hill. It looked majestic and scary in the night sky. "Are you sure we're not in Transylvania?" I asked softly, half-joking.

"No, no." He grinned. "Casper's ancestors were really into the gothic look."

"The castle looks scary," I said as we got out of the limo.

"Don't worry, no vampires are going to come out and bite you tonight, though I can't promise you that no teeth will be in your skin."

"Xavier!" A loud voice called out to us. I turned around to see who was coming, but could only make out the man's silhouette.

"Casper." Xavier's tone changed, and I watched him carefully. "It has been a while since I saw you last."

"I've been busy."

"So I've heard." The man stopped in front of us and I gasped as I stared up at his face. He was possibly the most handsome man I'd ever seen in my life. In fact, he was possibly so handsome that he was beautiful. He had the most vibrant blue eyes I'd ever seen, and his short blond hair was cropped low. He stood before me in a black tuxedo with a huge smile on his face. He bowed down and then reached for my hand and then kissed it.

"Hello, beautiful." He grinned at me. "I'm Casper."

"I'm Lola," I responded and swallowed hard. I could feel Xavier staring at me, but I couldn't take my eyes from Casper. He had really captivated me, and I could feel my heart beating, fast.

"Lola's with me." Xavier stepped forward and put his hand around my waist. His fingers pressed into my side, and I could feel the tension in the air.

"You always did have good taste." Casper continued smiling, but his eyes never left my face as he spoke.

"Yes, I have." Xavier's tone was dry. "Are we going to go inside?"

"Of course." Casper nodded. "The party is in full force. You both have your masks?"

"Yes." I spoke up and pulled the gold mask on so that it was covering my eyes.

"Beautiful." He smiled and I saw his eyes fall to my breasts.

"Thanks," I said back lightly as we walked through the castle doors. My eyes didn't know where to look as I looked around. There were no lights on in the castle. Every room had hundreds of candles providing light and I could see couples talking and walking around. I wasn't sure what sort of ball was held by candlelight, but maybe Casper was trying to save money on his electricity bill.

"Would you like a drink?" Casper escorted us up some steps and into a larger room with large plush couches. I could see a few couples kissing and I felt my face growing red. Was this normal in Europe? I was pretty sure one of the couples was having sex. She was on his lap and rocking back and forth and I was pretty confident she wasn't just dancing.

"I'll have a glass of wine, please." I nodded quickly and he smiled at me.

"Don't be overwhelmed." He leaned forward and whispered in my ear. "You'll find that the club is something to enjoy and not fear." I felt the tip of his tongue licking my ear before he pulled away quickly and I wasn't sure if he had done it on purpose or by mistake.

"Thanks."

"I'll have a scotch on the rocks." Xavier gave him his order and grabbed my arm and we walked over to an empty couch as Casper disappeared.

"Your friend Casper seems nice," I said shyly, feeling desperately out of place.

"He's not my friend." Xavier scowled.

"Then why did we come here?" I asked softly, but Xavier didn't hear me. "So, what is this place?" I asked in a louder voice. I looked around me and I could see people dancing, talking and kissing. However, all the women were in ball gowns and all the men were in tuxedos.

"I told you before, it's a club."

"A night club?" I shouted as the music grew louder.

"No." He shook his head. "It's a pleasure club."

"A pleasure club?" I repeated, confused.

"We teach women how to give us pleasure." He grinned at me and winked.

"What does that mean?" I sat back, my body feeling frozen.

"I'm joking. It's about mutual pleasure. How we can both make each other orgasm in as many ways as possible."

"This is a sex club?" I gasped in shock.

"No, no." He shook his head. "A sex club would be crass. We're princes, we're not crass. It's different ways for us to teach women alternative methods to pleasure us. Though there are some people that like to practice the techniques here. It's a judgment-free zone."

"So, you're telling me this club is for princes to teach their girlfriends how to please them in the bedroom?"

"No." He shook his head. "It's about a lot more than that. It's about brotherhood. It's about trust."

"Well, I don't think girls can be considered brothers."

"I mean the club is about brotherhood for all the princes." He shrugged. "It's a way for us to be tied together and bonded."

"By teaching women how to have sex?" I frowned. "Really?"

"We don't teach women how to have sex. Yes, there are classes where the women talk and discuss techniques, but no one is teaching you anything unless you want them to."

"Do you guys swap here?" I asked slowly, wondering if he was trying to pimp me out.

"Some men do. I do not." He grabbed my hands. "Remember, I am Alpha and you are Omega. No one comes between us. Whatever we try here, we try together."

"What are we going to try?"

"There are rooms." He grinned. "There are toys."

"What rooms and toys?"

"Today is day one, you don't need to learn everything tonight." His fingers traced up my arm and to my shoulder. "This dress is a perfect fit. It teases me." He glanced at my breasts. "I'm so close, we're all so close to seeing your beautiful breasts. The dress gives the illusion that one wrong move and your breasts will be on display. I've been waiting for that move."

"That's funny because that's a move I'm praying will not happen." My breath caught as his fingertips ran across my lips. He leaned forward to kiss my neck and then his lips burned a trail of fire down my chest and the valley between my breasts.

"So sorry to disturb you both." Casper walked back to us with our drinks. "Xavier, Prince Richard would like to talk to you."

"Now?" Xavier frowned as he pulled away from me.

"He wants to talk to you about the board. You never responded to his last letter."

"I'll talk to him later."

"He's leaving soon." Casper shrugged. "He wants to talk to you now. Don't worry about Lola. I'll look after her when you're gone, unless you don't trust me." There was silence in the air as the two men stared at each for a few seconds, but then Xavier stood up.

"I'll be right back." He looked at me for a few seconds and then left. Casper sat down next to me and I could feel his thigh pressing against mine. It felt warm and muscular, and I felt slightly guilty to be feeling so excited to have him sitting next to me.

"So you're the new girl Xavier's been dating?" he asked me softly and I nodded. "He always does find the best girls." His fingers ran down my arm and then stopped. "So tell me about yourself, Lola."

"What would you like to know?" I asked softly and took a swig of wine.

"First of all, what do you think of my home?"

"I haven't seen much of it, but it seems beautiful. The architectural details seem amazing." I looked around the room and then back at him.

"We have a lot of bedrooms here." He grinned and leaned forward and kissed my shoulder.

"Uhm, okay. What are you doing?" I moved back slightly taken aback. Was he coming on to me?

"Sorry. I couldn't resist. You're such a sexy girl."

"Why are you kissing me? You know I'm here with Xavier."

"It doesn't matter who you came with." He shrugged, his eyes dancing. "We princes share and share alike."

"What does that mean?"

"It means that if I find you attractive and you find me attractive, we can have some fun without anyone getting upset or jealous." He reached out and touched my hair. "Or didn't Xavier fully explain the club to you?"

"He just said it's a pleasure club." I frowned. "We didn't get to talk about it much." I shifted in the seat and the slit in my dress widened and exposed a large expanse of leg. I looked down and tried to move the dress over, but it wouldn't close.

"No need to be modest, Lola." Casper laughed and grabbed my hand. I could feel the warmth of his skin next to my leg. "You have beautiful legs." He pulled my hand up my thigh and then squeezed it slightly. "So silky, long and smooth." He said softly as he caressed my thigh. I sat there in shock, not sure how to feel. His hand felt warm and nice, and I waited for a couple of seconds before pushing it away.

"Thank you." I shifted away from him. "So who are you with?"

"Oh, she'll be here soon." Casper stared at me intently. "She's teaching a class right now."

"Oh?"

"Yes, she helps women get in touch with their feminine side. You'll have to join one of her next classes."

"Yes, yes, I will do that." *Yeah, right,* I thought to myself.

"So have you ever had a threesome?" Casper moved closer to me again and kissed my collarbone.

"No." I shook my head and looked around the room. Where had Xavier gone?

"Have you ever wanted to have a threesome?" His fingers ran along my shoulder and he trailed them down my arm again. It was at that moment that I felt the vibrator start to move gently. I looked around to see if I could locate Xavier, but I couldn't.

"No." I shook my head and shifted in my seat. That had been a mistake. I could now feel the vibrator even more intensely.

"I think you'd be surprised at how much fun they can be." Casper's hand was on my knee, and I could feel him running it up my leg. I was about to brush it away when the vibrator kicked up a notch.

"Oh, shit," I muttered as I felt it rubbing against my clit aggressively.

"Sorry, what?" Casper leaned back and his hand ran back to my knee.

"Nothing." I bit my lower lip and tried to ignore the feelings that were building up inside of me.

"Are you okay?" His eyes narrowed and he studied my face.

"I'm fine." I nodded and put my face in my hands. The vibrator was moving even faster now and I knew that I was about to orgasm any minute. Casper's hand was still on my leg and I felt it moving upward again. Only this time it wasn't stopping. His fingers seemed to move in pace with the vibrator and I was going crazy inside. I didn't know what to do. All I could think about was how close I was to coming. I felt his hand moving up higher and I reached down and grabbed it as I felt his fingers next to my panties. I held on to his hand to move it away when I felt my orgasm hit. My body shook for a few seconds as I came and I knew that he could feel the movement of the vibration next to his fingers.

"What do you think you're doing?" I gasped and jumped up. "How dare you?"

"How dare I?" He mocked me and smiled. "I'm sorry, I thought you wanted it."

"You thought I wanted your hands on me?"

"I was obviously mistaken." He jumped up and stood next to me. "Please accept my apologies. I think I got confused. You seemed like you were feeling horny, but I guess it wasn't because of me. You had other things to make you come."

"I, uh..." I looked away from him in embarrassment. I was going to kill Xavier when he returned. How dare he turn on the vibrator while I was with Casper? He had to know what was going to happen. Had this been his way of showing Casper that I was his woman?

"There you are, Casper." A familiar female voice walked over to us and I froze. "Who are you with?" The voice was suddenly next to me and I looked to the side. "Oh, it's you." Violeta looked at me in distaste.

"Hello." I nodded.

"We meet again." Violeta didn't look pleased as she pressed herself into Casper's arm and then gave him a kiss. "Have you missed me terribly, darling?"

"Of course," Casper's hand fell to her ass and squeezed as they kissed, his eyes never leaving mine.

"There you are." Xavier's voice was dry as he joined us. "Have you missed me?" His eyes were narrowed as he looked at me.

"You're a jerk," I whispered back at him.

"I took good care of her for you, Xavier." Casper pulled away from Violeta and smiled. "Or maybe that was all you." He laughed. "Someone had her all hot and bothered. I'm not sure if it was me or not."

Xavier pulled me into his arms and I stood there awkwardly as he and Violeta stared at each other for a few seconds. It was only now that I was facing her that I could see that her entire dress was completely sheer. Every part of her body was exposed and showed off her perfect figure.

"Violeta." Xavier nodded and she tossed her head and leaned forward and kissed him on the lips.

"Xavier," she said breathlessly. "Good to see you."

"Lola, come, let me get you another drink." Casper grabbed my hand before I could protest, and I walked with him reluctantly as we left Xavier and Violeta to talk.

***

His View

"It's good to see you, Xavier." Violeta smiled up at me as she pressed her breasts into my chest.

"I wish I could say the same." I pulled away from her slightly.

"I've missed you," she sighed, running her fingers down the front of my chest.

"You could have fooled me." I grabbed her hand and pushed her away.

"Who's the girl?" She batted her eyelashes at me. "She doesn't look like your type."

"It's none of your business." I shook my head.

"It's always my business," she whispered in my ear, and I felt her hand at the front of my pants, squeezing my crotch. "Does she know the games we used to play?"

"There's nothing for her to know."

"I think she'd be very interested in knowing the real reason why she's here." She laughed as she unzipped my pants and I grabbed her wrist.

"Get your hand off of me." I squeezed it tightly as I pulled her away from me. "You have no business touching me."

"You know that you still want me." She licked her lips and took a step back. "Let's not even play that game. Does she know that the last partner you had at the club was me?" She smiled and then winked. "And does she know the story of how it ended?"

"Shut up, Violeta," I growled at her and took a step back. "Leave me and Lola alone."

"I'll do my best." She leaned forward and kissed me on the lips. "Though you know, no one will ever compare to me." She licked my lips before biting down hard on my lower lip and stepping back. "I'll see you later." She walked away from me knowing I was watching after her as she swung her hips. I stood there immobile and angry. It had been a mistake to bring Lola here. She wasn't ready for the secrets and games that the club held. I wasn't sure why I'd thought it was a good idea. Well, that was wrong. I had brought Lola for a specific reason, but now I was beginning to doubt myself. I wasn't sure that it had been a good decision. This wasn't Lola's world. She had no idea what she was getting into by coming with me to the club. I thought back to what had happened before, and I knew that I was playing with fire. Only this time, the circumstances were different. This time, I knew exactly what could happen. I watched as Lola walked back to me with Casper, and I could feel the anger rising up inside of me. Why was she smiling at him? It annoyed me that she was so obviously captivated by his looks. I had hoped that she would be one of the women who wasn't taken in by his charm. I wanted to bring Casper down, but I wasn't sure if Lola was the right person to help me with the job. I had a bad feeling about bringing her here. I wasn't sure when I had started to grow a conscience, but I knew that I no longer felt like I had in

London. In London, I'd been captivated by being with Lola, I'd only wanted sex. And I'd wanted to get her out of my mind as soon as possible. Now I was starting to feel more for her. There was a bond there that was growing. A bond I didn't know if I wanted to grow, but I wasn't sure how to stop it. I felt my body burning up as she approached me with an unsure smile and Casper's hand on her waist. The games had already begun. I'd lit the match that had started the fire. Now, I just had to hope that I hadn't set off fireworks as well.

Chapter Seven

"This place is crazy," I whispered to Xavier as Casper finally left us alone.

"Do you want to leave?" Xavier studied my face, and I shook my head.

"No, it's fine." I bit my lower lip. "I'm kind of intrigued." I took another sip of wine, and I could tell that I was starting to feel light-headed.

"I see." Xavier looked disappointed, but I wasn't sure if I was imagining it. "Shall I show you around?"

"Yes, that would be great."

"Prince Richard would like to meet you." He nodded and grabbed my hand. "Let's go walk around."

"How do you know Violeta?" I asked softly, wondering if he would tell me.

"She's an old friend of the family." He shrugged and I sighed. Did that mean that she was Sebastian's old girlfriend, then? Did that confirm my suspicions or not?

"She's very beautiful," I said, trying again.

"Yes." He nodded. "She is."

"Casper must be so happy to be dating her."

"I think he is happy that he has her as a trophy, yes." He nodded. "Now let's stop talking about her."

"Okay," I sighed. "Why did you turn the vibrator on when I was talking to Casper? I thought you said you weren't going to use it."

"I said I would turn it on when I wanted you to think of me." He shrugged. "Forgive me. I had left you in the company of a ladies man. I know he likes to try his tricks. I wanted to ensure that you were thinking of me when I left."

"It was so embarrassing." I mumbled. "I had an orgasm on the chair."

"Oh?" He stopped and looked at me with a light in his eyes. "You did?"

"Yes, I did." I bit my lower lip. "And it feels uncomfortable now. I want to take it off."

"You can take it off if you take your panties off as well."

"What?" I shook my head. "No way."

"Remember, I'm the boss of you tonight." He laughed. "You take off your panties and then I'll let you take off your vibrator."

"Xavier," I sighed and reached up and touched his face. "Why do you delight in tormenting me? Why do I feel like this is all one big game to you? You tease me. You tantalize me. Now you want me to take off my panties."

"Yes, I want you to take off your panties." Then he stopped. "Actually that's not true, I want to take off your panties." He pulled me towards him and I felt his hands pulling my dress up slightly.

"What are you doing?" I gasped. "You can't just pull up my dress."

"Shh." He grinned and pushed me back towards the wall. "It's fine." He pulled my dress up and pulled my panties down quickly, before reaching up and unhooking the vibrator from the leg bands. His fingers lingered at my pussy for a few seconds and he grinned as he played with my wetness. "I see you really did come," he whispered in my ear, and I felt his hardness against me. "I want to fuck you so badly right now."

"Xavier." I pushed him away, feeling slightly horny. "I'm not having sex with you in a public room."

"So you do want to have sex?"

"I'm not saying anything," I groaned as I felt him push a finger inside of me. My body trembled at his touch and I reached up and played with his hair. Everything felt so surreal. Being with him felt dangerous and murky and extremely sensual.

"Come." He pulled away from me slightly, his finger leaving me as he pulled my dress back down. "Let me introduce you to Richard first."

"First?"

"Before we find a bedroom."

"Oh, okay." I grinned back at him. I think the wine must have gone to my head because I felt like a completely different person. Xavier grabbed my hand and escorted me out of the room and up another flight of stairs. This time we entered a smaller room that only had two couples. We walked over to the two couches that they were sitting on, and I was pleased to see that neither of the couples was making out or having sex.

"Richard, allow me to introduce Lola." Xavier grinned at his friend. "Lola, this is Prince Richard and his date, Elizabeth." Then he turned to the other couple. "And this is Prince George and his date, Victoria."

"Hi." I nodded at the couples feeling slightly shy. Prince Richard had to have been in his forties and his date was about my age. She looked young and happy, and I wondered why she was so excited. Prince Richard was not cute with his bald head and big belly.

"Hello, Lola." Richard jumped up and bowed before me. "It's a pleasure to meet you."

"You too." I smiled at him and then took a seat next to Elizabeth. "Hi." I smiled at her.

"Hi, nice to meet you." She grinned at me and I realized that she was American as well.

"Are you from the States?" I asked her curiously.

"Yeah, I'm from Texas. Austin to be exact."

"Oh, nice."

"Yeah, where are you from?"

"Florida."

"Oh, cool. I love Disney."

"Yeah, Disney is fun, but I prefer Universal Studios."

"I've never been to Universal." She smiled at me and I smiled back at her, thinking how crazy this was for us to be sitting in a 'pleasure club' talking about theme parks. "I do like Wet N' Wild, though." She grinned and I laughed.

"Yeah, I love water parks."

"Oh, I mean I like it when Richard makes me wet and wild." She laughed at her joke, and I tried not to roll my eyes. "Sorry, I've got a quirky sense of humor."

"No worries. So do I." I sat back and looked at Richard and Xavier talking intensely and then turned back to her. "So, have you been coming here long?"

"To the club, you mean?" She looked at me curiously. "Is this your first time?"

"Yes." I nodded, feeling embarrassed.

"Oh, wow. Okay." She grinned. "You must be so overwhelmed. I know I was when I first came with Richard."

"Yeah, I don't really know what's going on. Is this like a sex club?"

"No, not really." She shook her head.

"So people don't swap or anything?"

"No, no." She shook her head and looked shocked. "This isn't that sort of club at all."

"Oh, okay. Good. What about that Casper guy? Do you know him?"

"Oh, Prince Casper is gorgeous, isn't he?" She sighed. "Every girl here wishes she could be with him."

"He doesn't try and get with everyone?" I asked surprised.

"Oh, no." She shook her head. "He only brings the most beautiful women."

"Like Violeta?"

"Oh, you met her." Elizabeth made a face. "She's beautiful, but a bit of a bitch."

"Yes, she is." I laughed, glad that I wasn't the only one who thought that.

"She's one of the teachers here, so we have to be nice, but most of us girls can't stand her."

"She's a teacher here?" I asked, surprised. "Isn't she dating Casper?"

"I don't know. He doesn't really do much. I've never even really seen him kissing anyone." She shrugged. "He's a pretty closed-off guy. I think he only goes with the girls who he really, really likes."

"Oh, wow." I felt myself warming inside. What did that mean then? Did he like me? Why had he been flirting with me so hardcore? Did he really think I was beautiful?

"Yeah, he's a straight-up guy. Some of the guys will try and cop a feel." She rolled her eyes. "But not Casper." She sighed. "Most of us wouldn't mind if it was him."

"Yeah, he's really cute, isn't he?" I pictured his amazingly vibrant blue eyes and then the feel of his warm hand on my leg and blushed.

"Yeah, he is." Elizabeth giggled. "Though Prince Xavier is a tall glass of water as well."

"Yeah, he is." We sat back and looked at Xavier. He looked so distinguished in his suit. His dark hair was styled perfectly and his suit fit him like a glove. I stared at him as he spoke and I felt my heart turning. I loved this man with all his flaws and imperfections, yet I knew that he would never commit to me. He just wasn't interested in a relationship, and it killed me inside. I wasn't sure how long I'd be able to keep up the farce and not crack under pressure.

"Richard might not be cute, but he makes up for it in the bedroom." She laughed. "He's the best lover I've ever had."

"Oh, wow. That's amazing." I smiled at her and looked away from Xavier. I wasn't sure what else to say to her. She was definitely nice, but I knew she wasn't someone I could confide in.

"Yes, he is." She leaned towards me. "I'm sure you're wondering what you got yourself into, but trust me, just go with the flow. The club is a lot of fun. It's like a pleasure palace. You can learn how to give and receive as much pleasure as you want. And pain." She giggled.

"Pain?" I frowned. "What?"

"Oh, if you guys go into the bondage rooms, they have some whips and chains and other stuff. And this wheel that spins, that was crazy."

"Yeah, it sounds it."

"It's not all pain." She smiled at me and stood up. "In fact, the slight pain helps to intensify the pleasure even more. If you have a chance you should go up to that level. It's exciting."

"Yeah, I'll see." I stood up as well and she gave me a quick hug.

"It was nice meeting you, Lola. Have fun and relax. I think I'm going to take Richard to one of the shows now." She walked away from me and over to the two talking men. I stood there wondering what show she was talking about and smiled as Xavier approached me.

"Sorry about that." He apologized as he looked down at me. "Richard and I were just talking business."

"That's fine." I shrugged. "I was talking to Elizabeth. She seems really nice."

"Yes, she's a nice girl." He nodded. "Are you ready for us to go and have some fun?"

"I guess so," I said as we walked out of the room. "Where are we going?"

"Where do you want to go?"

"I don't know." I shook my head. "I don't really know this place well."

"True." He laughed. "Follow me, then. I know where we can go." We walked up another flight of stairs and then down a long dark corridor before we stopped and he pushed open a door. There was a huge bed in the middle and he picked me up and plopped me down on the bed. I looked around the room and then up at him.

"Are you sure this is a good room to be in? It looks as if someone actually sleeps in this room."

"It's fine." He pulled his shirt off and threw it to the ground before unzipping his pants. "Come here," he growled as he jumped onto the bed next to me and pulled my dress off. I lay on the bed completely naked and watched as he pulled his briefs off. His cock was already hard, and I moaned as he bent down and took my nipple in his mouth and sucked.

"Xavier!" I cried out as I scratched his back and closed my eyes. It felt so surreal to be in this castle, in this strange room, naked and ready to make love. A part of me was screaming at myself, wondering what I was doing. How could I be here right now? This was so out of my comfort zone it wasn't funny, but it was so exhilarating and exciting at the same time.

"I've wanted to do this all night," he groaned as he kissed down my stomach and spread my legs open.

His mouth found my quivering pussy and he licked me eagerly and quickly. His tongue entered me as he sucked on my clit and my body trembled as my legs shook on his face. He ate me out eagerly—as if he hadn't eaten food for a year and this was the best meal he'd ever tasted. I ran my hands to his hair and pulled it slightly as I felt myself coming.

As soon as I'd finished having my first orgasm, Xavier kissed back up to my lips and then reached down and grabbed a piece of material from the floor.

"I want you to wear this as I fuck you," he muttered in my ear. "Or rather as you fuck me."

"What?"

"I want you to ride me," he groaned as he tied the material around my face, covering my mask so that I couldn't see. I sat up and I was about to straddle him, when he grabbed my hips.

"No, I want you to face the other way." He swiveled me around, and I rubbed myself back and forth on his cock slowly as I faced the way of the door. My ass was facing his face and I felt him squeezing it as his cock slid in-between my legs. I sat up slightly and lowered myself onto him, groaning as he filled me up.

"Oh shit, you feel so good," he muttered as he grabbed my hips and I started moving back and forth even faster. "You're so sexy," he groaned and that made me increase my pace.

**

His View

Lola moved back and forth on my cock quickly and I could feel her wetness on my legs. My hands moved up to cup her breasts as she rode me, and I grinned when I heard the door opening slightly. I looked up and saw Casper and Violeta standing there looking in at us. I reached my right hand down to Lola's clit and rubbed it as she rode me. She cried out as I rubbed her faster and faster. She had no idea that we were being watched as she rode me with abandon. Casper's eyes narrowed as he made eye contact with me, and I gave him a wide smile as I felt Lola's pussy lips contracting on my cock. She was about to come and I knew she was going to scream. I felt a surge in power in me as a few seconds later; she was riding me faster and faster and crying out her pleasure as I fucked her in Casper's bed. Casper and Violeta stared at me with narrowed eyes before they closed the door, and I was then able to relax and come even more. Round two had definitely gone to me.

"That was so good." Lola collapsed back on the bed next to me and pulled off the tie and her mask as she stared at me. "It was almost magical."

"Yes, it definitely was." I grinned back at her and kissed her firmly, trying to ignore the feelings of guilt that were rising up in me. I knew that Lola wouldn't have been happy if she knew that Casper and Violeta had watched her fucking me. Normally, I wouldn't have cared, but something about her and being with her was making me regret everything I had set in motion.

Chapter Eight

I woke up in my bed back at Xavier's palace, and I had no idea how I'd gotten there. The last thing I could remember was cuddling with Xavier after the hot sex we'd had.

"Wakey wakey, Lola." Xavier's voice next to me made me smile and I looked over at him.

"When did we come back?"

"A few hours ago." He smiled. "You fell asleep and I waited for you to wake up, but then I realized you were out for the night, so I just picked you up and carried you to the car and then the plane."

"Wow, I can't believe I didn't wake up."

"Neither could I." He laughed and kissed my shoulder. "We should get up, though. We're going to be having lunch with Richard."

"Oh, fun." I jumped out of bed and stretched. I was wearing my shorts and a T-shirt. I was surprised that Xavier hadn't left me naked. "I like Elizabeth, she seems fun."

"Yeah." He nodded and paused. "I'm not sure that she'll be there today."

"Oh, sad." I made a face. "It would have been nice to see her, but I suppose you and Richard will be fine."

"There might be some other people there." He got out of bed and ran his hands through his hair. "Why don't you go and shower, and I'll call down and have some breakfast sent up."

"Okay, sure." I nodded and walked to the bathroom, feeling sore and disappointed. My body could still remember the events of last night and I was sad that we weren't going to repeat our performance in the shower. I groaned as I stepped under the hot water. What was happening to me? I was starting to feel like I'd stepped into a movie and I wasn't sure what character I was playing. This whole situation was so foreign to me. I grabbed the soap and bathed myself, smiling as I thought about Xavier. And then I remembered Casper. What had that been all about? I frowned as I remembered his light kiss and touch. He'd definitely been flirting with me. It had felt sort of nice as well. He'd been a really attractive guy, but I'd been uncomfortable in the situation and was still slightly annoyed with Xavier. I didn't know if I was coming or going with him. Sometimes he could be so sweet and loving and then other times, he was just very standoffish. I truly didn't know what he thought about me and that concerned me. Did he like me? Did he only want me for sex? Was he falling for me? Where exactly did I stand? I also wanted to ask him, why the fake engagement? It still didn't make sense to me. However, I was scared that he might react in a way that would hurt me. If he did, I might end up crying and then he might end up realizing that I was falling in love with him. I couldn't stand for him to know that I was starting to develop feelings for him, especially as he'd made it clear that he didn't do feelings. I thought back to the man I'd known in London. He'd been so rude and yet so thoughtful when he'd showed me around the museum. And then we'd traveled to Paris and I'd felt like I was in a fairytale. The man from the classroom—the man who was my professor—was very different to the man who was my lover and fake fiancé in Romerius.

I sighed as I scrubbed my skin. I was so confused and the world was topsy turvy. I had a weird feeling in my stomach all of a sudden. I felt like I was in too deep and the saddest part was, I didn't even really know what I was in.

***

"Maxine's is one of the hottest restaurant's in Romerius." Xavier and I walked alongside a beautiful redhead that was escorting us to our table. "Every time, Richard comes to visit, he wants to eat here."

"Oh, does he come to Romerius a lot, then?" I asked surprised. It had seemed like they hadn't spoken to each other in ages at the party the previous evening.

"I wouldn't say a lot, no." He shook his head and then stopped at the table where Richard was sitting next to a middle-aged lady. "Richard, Charlotte, good to see you both. It's been too long."

"Xavier." Richard reached out and shook his hand and then Xavier kissed Charlotte's cheek.

"This is Lola, Lola meet Prince Richard and his beautiful wife, Charlotte." He nodded towards me and I smiled at them both weakly. What in hell was going on here? Richard was married? So who was Elizabeth, then? And why hadn't Xavier told me?

"Hi, nice to meet you both." I nodded and shook their hands and slid into the chair, Xavier had pulled out for me.

"It's very nice to meet you, Lola. We've heard a lot about you." Charlotte smiled at me broadly as I sat down.

"Oh, really?" I looked at her in surprise.

"Yes, we know that you love art as well," Richard spoke up, the expression in his eyes light and unconcerned, as if he were positive I wasn't going to ask him why he was with a girl called Elizabeth last night and a wife called Charlotte today.

"Yes, I do love art." I smiled. "Xavier was actually my professor in London." I spoke sweetly and picked up the menu. My head was starting to pound. I could sense that Xavier was looking at me, but I didn't look up. Just when I thought we were starting to get on the right track, something would happen that made me doubt him and his sincerity all over again.

"Now that I didn't know." Charlotte laughed, and I looked up at her. She was smiling at me genuinely and I smiled back, feeling guilty inside that I knew her husband was cheating on her.

"I guess that's not something Xavier cares to share with everyone." I giggled and then looked at him. "Isn't that true, honey?" His eyes narrowed as he stared at me, and I knew he could tell something was off. I hoped that he was worried that I'd blurt out more information. How could he think it was okay to not tell me that Richard and his wife would be here, especially after I had mentioned Elizabeth? Did he think that this was cool or right? I knew men were different and he was different, but I just did not agree with cheating.

"I don't mind if people know you were in my class," he said smoothly. "Just like I don't mind people knowing you slept with me on the first date. I thought it was you who wanted to keep those things a secret."

"I'm fine," I said stiltedly, my face growing red.

"Xavier, stop teasing the poor girl," Charlotte chided him and reached for my hand. "You must ignore him, Lola. Xavier loves to rile people up."

"No, I don't," he retorted. "I just like to have some fun."

"Maybe too much fun," Richard answered with a wry smile. "I heard what you were up to last night."

"Whatever do you mean?" Xavier grinned.

"Casper's room, Xavier?" Richard shook his head and laughed.

"What are you two talking about?" Charlotte asked the question I was thinking and they both shook their heads.

"Nothing of importance." Xavier smiled smugly. "I just had a message I wanted to give Casper last night, and I left it in his room."

"Oh yes, he had that party that you went to." She looked at her husband. "You and your boys club parties." She shook her head and looked at me. "Something for you to look forward to Lola. When you marry Xavier, he'll be out and about with his friends and you'll be stuck at home with the babies, while he does who knows what."

"Parties?" I asked softly, afraid to look at Richard and Xavier.

"Yes, they all get together and play poker and talk politics." Charlotte smiled and took a sip of water. "Only no women are allowed."

"Oh." I answered her softly and grabbed my water glass as well.

"No wives allowed." Richard rubbed her hand. "You'd ruin the mood, honey."

"I told you I could learn poker." Charlotte turned to him, completely not getting what his 'no wives' allowed comment was about. She had no idea she wasn't allowed to go because he was actually going to sleep with another woman. Then it hit me. Maybe that was the point of the club. Maybe it was for the mistresses. Maybe that's why everything was so mysterious. My heart started thudding then because I realized that if Xavier was taking me there, he had no intentions of ever becoming more serious with me. I was just his play toy. An object of desire. He had no real feelings for me and never would.

"It's about more than playing poker, Charlotte. It's about bonding." Richard sighed. "I've told you this before."

"Excuse me, please." I jumped up out of my seat. "I need to go to the ladies room." I walked away from the table quickly, not wanting to listen to him lie to his wife any longer. I walked to the front of the restaurant and then slipped outside to the main road so that I could get some fresh air on my face.

"What are you doing?" Xavier's voice sounded angry next to me.

"I came to get some air. Is that a problem?"

"Why would it be a problem?" He shrugged and looked into my eyes. "Are you okay?"

"What do you think?" My voice rose. "You brought me to lunch with a man and his wife. A man I met last night with his girlfriend."

"So?" He shrugged.

"You don't think that's shady?"

"It's not my life. Not my relationship. What Richard does is his business."

"That's horrible." I shook my head and turned away from him. "You're a pig."

"I'm a pig because Richard has a mistress?"

"You're a pig because you can't see that what he's doing is wrong."

"Lots of married men have mistresses."

"And they are all pigs as well."

"I think I'm a good guy." He paused. "I have no plans to marry, so I will never have a mistress."

"Oh wow, great for you." I said sarcastically. "That makes everything so much better."

"I'm just being honest. I know you're not seriously mad at me for not telling you he was married, are you?"

"Yes, I am upset. In fact, I'm pissed. How could you not tell me?" I hissed. "Especially as I mentioned Elizabeth this morning."

"I know, I should have said something." He sighed and came closer to me. "I knew you would be upset."

"So why are you acting surprised now?"

"I was hoping you wouldn't overreact."

"Overreact. I'm an accomplice now." I bit my lower lip. "How can I look her in the face knowing I was having a conversation with someone last night who was telling me how good Richard was in bed. Someone who is not his wife."

"I'm sorry, I realize this is a delicate situation for you."

"Delicate doesn't even begin to cover it. This is awkward." I sighed. "This is more than awkward. I'm a fake fiancée meeting a man and his wife, when I was just hanging out with his mistress."

"Keep your voice down, Lola." He frowned. "I get it. You're upset. We will talk later."

"I don't want to talk later. And by that I mean if you think talk means sex, you're going to be waiting a long time. I don't sleep with pigs."

"Lola, grow up." His voice was mad. "You're blowing this out of proportion."

"I really don't think I am." I shook my head. "I think that I'm as upset as any other caring human being would be. Cheating is wrong."

"And I'm not saying it's good." He grabbed my hands. "Look at me. I don't agree with Richard's choices, but it is not for us to judge him."

"So you think it's wrong of him to commit adultery?" I asked softly, slightly mollified.

"Yes, I think it's wrong," he sighed and kissed me lightly on the lips. "I do not believe in adultery."

"Okay, then." I stared into his eyes to see if he was telling the truth. "That's good then because I don't believe in it, either."

"Can we go inside now?" he asked me softly. "They will be wondering what happened."

"I'm not cool with this, you know. I'd rather go back to the palace." I let out a deep sigh. "But I'll stay for a quick lunch. However, I'm telling you now, if you do something like this again, I won't be so patient and I won't go along with it."

"Duly noted," he said with a small smile on his face. "I'm glad to hear you stick to your principles."

"I do, and you better not forget it." I gave him a look and he nodded slightly as he took in my angry appearance.

"I don't think I'll forget."

***

"I'm going up to the room." I said to Xavier as we arrived back at the palace after the lunch. "I need a shower to wash the shame off of me."

"Lola, no need to be so melodramatic."

"Whatever." I shuddered, thinking back to the farce of a lunch. Charlotte had spent most of the hour talking about what a good husband Richard was, and I'd felt so sorry for her. I hurried up the stairs and was walking down the corridor when I saw Tarquin.

"Oh, you're back." Tarquin grinned at me. "I have something for you."

"For me?" I frowned. "What?"

"Well, it's from Violeta." He shrugged. "She dropped it off this morning with a card. I guess she wanted to apologize."

"Oh, really?" I said doubtfully.

"Yes, hold on. Let me go and get it from my room." He ran back down the corridor, and I waited patiently, wondering what Violeta had bought for me. I really didn't believe she was going to apologize to me—and a gift as well? Something seemed off, but maybe Xavier or Casper had talked to her and told her to be nicer to me. "Here we go." He walked back with a small box wrapped in silver paper and a cream envelope. "I wonder what she got you."

"I'll let you know later, when I open it." I took the box and card from him. "Excuse me, I'm going to go and lie down now."

"Oh, okay." He looked disappointed. "Maybe we can hang out later."

"Yeah, that sounds good."

"Oh, I forgot to tell you. Sebastian is coming back to Romerius."

"What?" I was surprised. "When?"

"As soon as he can get a flight." He grinned.

"No private plane for him?"

"It's a surprise." Tarquin grinned. "No one knows except me and, well, you now."

"Oh, wow. Why is he coming back?"

"That's for me to know and you to find out." He grinned and flicked his blond hair. "I'll see you later."

"Yeah, okay." I nodded and walked back to the room, wondering why it was such a secret. However, Sebastian soon left my mind as I wanted to know what Violeta had gotten me. I ripped open the box eagerly and my jaw dropped when I saw a vibrator in the box that looked very similar to the one Xavier had given me. I dropped it on the floor and ripped open the envelope and read the card slowly.

Lola,

I heard about your fun last night with Xavier. Just thought you should know that you're not the first girl he's taken to the club with a vibrator. It's a fetish of his. The one in the box is the one he gave me when we were together. Yes, I'm the girl he was dating who broke his heart. I moved on to bigger and better. I'm sure you'd agree that Casper is a much better-looking man. Unfortunately, Xavier is still a bit upset and jealous that I left him. I suppose that's why he proposed to you and brought you to the club. Only thing is, that doesn't make me jealous. Just sad for him and sad for you. Next time you feel like taking a ride, it might help you to remember that there have been many other riders before you. And some of us were treated to gallops, not trots.

XOXO

Violeta

I read the letter twice unable to believe what I was reading. So Violeta wasn't Sebastian's ex, she was Xavier's ex? I suddenly felt like everything was clicking into place. Was Xavier using me to make Violeta jealous? Was that the real reason he'd brought me here to Romerius? I sat on the bed with the letter in my hand and read it again and then ripped it up into little pieces and lay back and stared at the ceiling waiting for Xavier to enter the room.

***

His View

I knew as soon as I opened the door that Lola was still upset. I hadn't thought she was going to react so badly to Richard being married, though it made me admire and respect her more. Lola was the girl I didn't think existed any more. She was the sort of girl I would want to meet if I believed in love.

"You okay?" I asked as I turned the light on and she sat up. Her face was red and blotchy and I could tell that she'd been crying. "What's wrong?" I frowned as I walked over to her. "You're not seriously crying because of Richard and Charlotte, are you?"

"No. I'm not crying about that." She gave me a look that was void of emotion and I froze in fear.

"Then what's wrong?"

"You used to date Violeta?" she spat out. "You used to take her to the club?"

"How do you know that?" I stepped forward.

"She sent me the vibrator you gave her."

Fuck! I should have known Violeta would do something like that.

"Don't you have anything to say?" She jumped up with her finger pointed at me. "How could you?"

"How could I?" I could feel my blood starting to boil. "I can do what I want. Yes, I used to fuck Violeta, what concern is it of yours? That was my past, Lola." I knew I sounded angry, but I was filled with fear. Would Lola leave me now? The sudden emptiness that hit me at the thought scared me.

"I met her and she was rude to me and you never even told me." She glared at me. "I thought I was—"

"You thought you were what?" I cut her off. "Haven't I told you many times that this is not real? We're not really engaged, Lola. I'm not your Prince Charming. We both know this is about our chemistry together. This is about the sex." I said bluntly as I stuck the knife into her heart. I could see the pain in her eyes as I spoke, but I was doing this for her as well as myself. I didn't want her to think I was someone I wasn't. I couldn't make her happy. I could never be the man she wanted me to be. I'd already brought her here under false pretenses. If she knew everything, she would hate me. I knew I should tell her everything. I knew I owed her the truth. The complete and utter truth. But the fact of the matter was I was scared. I didn't want to lose her, not yet. Not now. I couldn't let go of her. I knew that I was losing her with my words, but I didn't know how to stop hurting her. I didn't know how to warn her to stay away from me without having her leave. I didn't want her to leave. Not yet. I ignored the voice in my head that told me, *not ever*.

"I know we're not engaged for real," she retorted angrily, the fire back in her eyes as she glared at me. I stared at her beautiful face and felt my heart crying out for her. I was so confused. I didn't even know what I was thinking or feeling anymore.

"I'm sorry, though." I grabbed her hands. "I didn't mean to hurt you. I should have told you, but I wasn't sure you would want to know about my past."

"I don't know that I would have wanted to know either, but Violeta made sure that I did."

"I'll speak to her tonight." I frowned, angry that Violeta was playing her old games again. Yes, we'd been lovers and yes, I'd enjoyed being with her until I'd seen how manipulative she was.

"Tonight?"

"At the ball."

"The ball?" she groaned. "Another one?"

"Yes, I thought you enjoyed it last night."

"It was fine." She frowned. "This is the last one, though. I think we need to talk tomorrow. Like, really talk. I think I'm ready to go home."

"I see." I turned away from her, pain searing my heart. This was it then. She was going to leave. "It is what it is. Tonight we'll have one last night of fun and then tomorrow, tomorrow we can talk about you leaving."

The words sounded odd to my ears as I said them. I already knew that tonight was going to be explosive. I could feel it in my bones. I didn't know what was going to go down, and a part of me wondered if it was a good idea to go to the club again, but I dismissed my doubts. There was one room Lola hadn't seen yet. One room that might make her change her mind and stay. It was risky, but I had to at least try to keep her here. The only problem was I no longer knew why I wanted her to stay. Was it to help me carry out my plan or was it because I was starting to fall for her?

Chapter Nine

The plane ride back to Delmar was quiet. I had nothing to say to Xavier and he didn't bother trying to flirt with me. He was also smart enough to not bring up the vibrator again. I don't think I would ever look at a vibrator again in the same way. I'd sure not be able to use one without thinking about him and Violeta. I was still so angry and hurt, and I was mad at myself for going back to the club with him. The problem was that I didn't want him to know just how hurt I was by his words. I didn't want him to think that he'd devastated me as much as he had.

He was correct in what he'd said. He'd never led me to believe that this was more than sex. He'd let me know several times that he wasn't interested in anything else. It was my own fault that I'd believed that we were developing a deeper relationship. He'd never led me to believe anything else. I'd come tonight because of pride. I'd come because I didn't want him to know how hurt I was. Though I really just wanted to go home.

We disembarked the plane and walked to the limousine in silence. We drove up to Casper's castle without looking at each other. I stepped out of the car and shivered in the cool night air as I stared up at the dark building in front of us.

"Are you going to ignore me all night?" Xavier's voice was husky as we stood there.

"No." I stared straight ahead and we started walking forward.

"There you are." Casper and Violeta walked out of the castle with huge smiles.

"Good evening." I smiled at them both. I was not going to let that bitch know that she had affected me in any way.

"Nice to see you again, Lola." She smiled widely. "Been doing any trotting lately?"

"No." I smiled back at her. "I wore my stallion out, so he needed a break."

"Huh? What are you two talking about?" Xavier frowned, and I shook my head and grabbed a hold of his hand.

"Nothing." I pressed myself into him. "Let's go and get a drink."

"Oh, Lola, I was hoping you'd be a part of my class tonight." Violeta stepped in front of us. "Please say yes."

"I think she'll pass." Xavier's voice was curt and I frowned.

"No, actually I think I'll go. I think it'll be fun."

"Are you sure?" His eyes narrowed and he looked displeased.

"I'm sure." I let go of his hand and kissed him on the lips. "I'll see you later."

"Okay." He frowned, but he didn't stop me as I walked away with Violeta.

"Did you like my present?" she asked me softly as we walked down a dark hallway.

"Oh, it was great. Thank you. Really thoughtful of you."

She frowned at my response but didn't say anything as she opened a door. There were about five other girls in the room waiting for her and she smiled.

"Okay, girls. Tonight, I'm going to teach you the art of stripping."

"Like lap dances?" one girl called out, and Violeta rolled her eyes.

"No. I mean the art of taking your clothes off and turning your man on without even touching him. Anyone can sit on a guys' lap and get his cock hard. That's easy. You have to have real power to turn a man on just by stripping." She walked over to the side of the room. "I want to teach you girls that power. I'll show you an example and then each one of you will strip and show us your most seductive dance."

"No way," one girl called out. "That's too embarrassing."

"You can all wear masks," Violeta sighed. "That way you can pretend it's just you and your man in the room. Is that better?"

"Yeah, I guess so," the girl called back, and Violeta walked over to the corner of the room and turned some music on.

"Okay, everyone, watch me. Then you guys can have a turn." We all sat on some couches in the corner of the room, while some music started playing. Violeta's eyes glazed over and we all watched as she stripped her clothes off slowly and flung them to the ground. We all gasped as she stood there naked playing with her breasts and dancing. I couldn't believe what she was doing until she finished and opened her eyes. She looked directly at me as she spoke.

"Now that's how a real woman turns her man on. She isn't afraid to show him what's she's got going on." She squeezed her breasts together. "Men are visual creatures. When a man sees me touching my breasts, he starts to wish that he was the one touching them." She stepped back and pulled her clothes back on. It was then I realized she hadn't been wearing a ball gown like the rest of us.

"How are we supposed to strip with our dresses on?" I called out and she turned to me with a tight smile.

"I have outfits out here in the corner," she said. "Why don't you go first, Lola? You can choose an outfit and then I'll blindfold you. In fact, we can even change rooms to give you more space."

"Change rooms?" I frowned. "What?"

"Go and choose your outfit," one of the girls called out. "My man is waiting on me. I don't have all day for this lesson."

"Fine." I jumped up and walked over to Violeta. I looked down in her bag and looked through the clothes she had on offer. I didn't see anything I liked and debated what to do. I didn't even want to strip, but I wasn't going to let her get the better of me. "You know what? I'll just strip my bra and panties off," I said finally.

"Are you sure?" Violeta stared at me with a blank expression and I nodded.

"Yes, I'm sure."

"Okay, then, take your dress off and then I'll blindfold you and lead everyone to the new room. Once you hear the music, you can start."

"Fine." I nodded, my heart beating fast. I pulled my dress off quickly and stood there in my bra and panties feeling really exposed. What was I doing? Anna would think I had lost my mind if she saw me.

"You're ready?" she asked as she looked my body over. I felt very uncomfortable standing in front of her almost naked, but I knew I had to get over it.

"Yes."

"Good." She slipped something over my face and I was suddenly in darkness. "Stand up everyone," she called out and grabbed my arm. "We're going to go to a room with better acoustics."

"Okay," the girls chorused, and I walked slowly out of the room, letting Violeta lead the way. Every fiber in my body was screaming at me and telling me to run away, but I didn't. I had to prove to her that she didn't get to me. I wasn't going to allow her to think that she could unnerve me.

"Okay, we're here." She opened a door and we stepped into a warmer room. She walked me to some part of the room and stopped. "Stay here. You can start your act when the music starts. Don't take your blindfold off until you're done."

"Fine," I muttered back.

"And don't feel bad if you're not as sexy as me. Many women aren't as comfortable with their bodies as I am. Don't feel the need to touch your breasts if you're shy." And then I heard her walking away. I listened as the girls took their seats and I could feel my skin burning up as I stood there trembling. I was about to pull the blindfold off and run away when the music started. At first I felt pretty timid as I swung my hips back and forth, but as I got into the music, I found myself enjoying it more. I pretended that the only one watching me was Xavier. I removed my bra slowly, one strap at a time and dropped it to the ground. The cool air hit my breasts and hardened my nipples, but still I continued. This time I slipped my panties off quickly and threw them up in the air, all the while shaking my hips to the beat of the music.

I was starting to feel a rush of power as I stood there naked. I imagined Xavier staring at me, feeling turned on and I started playing with my breasts. I could imagine the look on his face as I squeezed my nipples. Then I had an idea. An idea that would put Violeta's striptease in the water. I ran my fingers down my body and lightly slipped them between my legs and rubbed myself. I was already wet. I grinned to myself as I thought about Xavier's face if he saw me doing that. The next thing I knew I was lowering myself to the ground and spreading my legs, my finger rubbing myself gently. I was really getting into it, when I heard light clapping. I froze as I remembered that the girls were in the room with me. I quickly jumped up and pulled my blindfold off.

I froze as I stared in front of me. There were about ten men sitting in front of me with the girls. Dead center sat Casper, and he was grinning at me from ear to ear. I heard a door open and looked to the side. Xavier was walking in with Violeta and his eyes widened when he saw me standing there completely naked.

"What are you doing, Lola?" His voice was angry as he walked over to me.

"I didn't know..." I started and then stopped at the look he was giving me. I felt ashamed of myself and upset and wanted to cry.

"Xavier, we should talk." Violeta tapped him on the shoulder as I bent down to pick up my bra and panties.

"Violeta, not now."

"It's important, Xavier," she continued. "Very important."

"Xavier," I touched his arm. "I want to go now."

He looked at me with thin lips and sighed. "Give me a second." He turned to Violeta and I could hear him whispering something to her. My body went into a shocked state. I couldn't believe he was doing this to me.

"Are you okay?" Casper jumped up onto the stage and grabbed my arm. "You look upset."

"I'm fine." I pulled away from him, wanting to be alone.

"Do you want to put some clothes on?" His voice was soft and soothing. "Come with me. Let Xavier and Violeta do their thing. They are always playing these games with each other. They shouldn't have involved you."

"What are you talking about?" I frowned, and he sighed.

"They joined the club together and they both like to do things that make the other one jealous. It was wrong of Xavier to bring you here. You seem like a great girl. Honestly, you're the sort of girl I would want to date."

"Oh?" I looked up at his handsome face as we left the room and remembered what Elizabeth had said about him not dating much.

"You're so beautiful and kind." He put his arm around my shoulders and rubbed my back. "You deserve better than Xavier Van Romerius."

"I don't understand why he just left me there and went to talk with her." I said angrily as he led me down a hallway. "Where are we going?"

"To my room so you can put on some clothes and relax." His fingers were now rubbing my lower back and I wondered if I was making a mistake. "Here we are." He opened a door and then closed it. "Have a seat on the bed and I'll see what I can find for you to wear."

"Thanks." I smiled at him and sat down and looked around the room. "This is your bedroom?" I frowned as I recognized it from my night with Xavier.

"Yes, why?"

"No reason." I bit down on my lip, wondering if this was part of Xavier's game as well.

"Are you okay?" Casper sat on the bed next to me and ran his fingers across my stomach. "Would you like me to give you a massage to relieve some stress?"

"No." I shook my head, feeling tears of confusion ready to fall.

"It might help." He sat behind me, and I felt his palms on my shoulders massaging me. I closed my eyes and let him work his magic as we sat there in the silence. It felt good, and I just needed to take my mind off of what had happened.

"I'm so embarrassed," I groaned as I sat there. "I can't believe I just gave everyone a striptease."

"The best part was when you played with yourself," he whispered into my ear. "And you shouldn't be embarrassed about that. That was the best part."

"Don't," I groaned, remembering everything. "I don't want to think about it."

"Maybe I can think of a way to help you feel better." He stopped massaging me and I felt his lips on my neck.

"What are you doing?" I frowned as he reached his hands around to cup my breasts over my bra.

"You know Violeta and Xavier are most probably in a closet fucking right now." His fingers slipped under my bra and squeezed my nipples. "Why shouldn't we have some fun as well?"

"I can't do that." I pulled away from him and stood up. "I'm sorry. You're handsome, but I can't."

"What about if it was more than just me, then?" He stood up and I stared at him in confusion.

"What do you mean?" I frowned at him and heard the door open. I turned around to see who was there and I gasped.

"You." My jaw dropped as a new man walked into the room with a small smile and locked the door behind him.

"Are you ready to have some fun?" He grinned at me and I stared back at him in shock, my heart beating fast. I felt Casper's hand rubbing my ass and I swallowed hard as he pulled me into his arms. I looked up at him for a second, unsure of what I should do. A part of me believed that Xavier was still in love with Violeta and wanted to be with her. Maybe Casper was right and they were fucking right now. If that was true, then what was stopping me from sleeping with Casper?

***

His View

"Violeta, I know what you sent Lola." My voice was angry as I shouted at her. "And I know that you're most probably behind that little stripping stunt." I banged my fist against the wall behind her and she flinched.

"You know you've missed me." She reached for my cock and I yanked her hand away.

"Do not touch me." I glared at her. "It is over and it's been over. I do not care about you."

"You want to be with me." Her eyes narrowed and I could see the evil in her eyes.

"Violeta, you were nothing but a fuck buddy to me. You had your fun, and then you fucked Casper. You're the lowest of the low. The fact that you would cheat on me with my cousin shows me that." I shook my head and laughed. "All this time, I'd been so angry and insulted, but I see you for who you really are. Yes, you're beautiful and yes, we had hot sex, but it meant nothing to me." I shook my head as it hit me. "But thank you. It's because of you that I realize that I have a relationship with the best girl in the world. It's because of you that I realize that I love Lola." My heart started beating rapidly as I realized the truth of my words. I loved her. I loved her, and I'd nearly lost her.

"I have to go and tell her how I feel." I shook my head and stepped back from a dazed-looking Violeta. "Thank you for making me realize how stupid I've been. I've been judging Lola since day one because of something you did. I realize I was wrong. She is beautiful inside and out. She would never cheat on me. She has integrity. She sees through the likes of someone like Casper. Lola is my gem. The jewel of my heart. She's the one I'm meant to be with. I know I can trust her with my heart." With that I spun around and headed out of the room. I needed to find her and apologize. I needed to tell her how wrong I'd been about everything. I needed her to know that I wanted this engagement to be real.

Author's Note

Thank you for reading *Taming My Prince Charming*. There will be one more book in the series called *Keeping My Prince Charming*. *Keeping My Prince Charming* will be out in September 2014.

Please join my MAILING LIST to be notified as soon as new books are released and to receive teasers (http://jscooperauthor.com/mail-list/). I also love to interact with readers on my Facebook page, so please join me here: https://www.facebook.com/J.S.Cooperauthor. You can find links and information about all my books here: http://jscooperauthor.com/books/!

As always, I love to here from new and old fans, please feel free to email me at any time at jscooperauthor@gmail.com.

List of J. S. Cooper Books

Scarred

Healed

The Last Boyfriend

The Last Husband

Before Lucky

The Other Side of Love

Zane & Lucky's First Christmas

Crazy Beautiful Love

The Ex Games 1, 2 and 3

The Private Club 1, 2 and 3

.

About the Author

J. S. Cooper was born in London, England and moved to Florida her last year of high school. After completing law school at the University of Iowa (from the sunshine to cold) she moved to Los Angeles to work for a Literacy non profit as an Americorp Vista. She then moved to New York to study the History of Education at Columbia University and took a job at a workers rights non profit upon graduation.

She enjoys long walks on the beach (or short), hot musicians, dogs, reading (duh) and lots of drama filled TV Shows.

Made in the USA
Charleston, SC
01 July 2015